"I don't want to kill you.

Just leave me be and let me return to my life."

"Can't do that." He took another step, and then another.

She squeezed the trigger.

Nick reacted quickly, diving to his left, but he wasn't quick enough.

Buckshot sprayed out of the gun, striking him in the leg. Blinding pain seared through his thigh. He hit the ground hard.

Ellie screamed. She stood on the porch, frozen, her hands locked around the gun. Tears welled in her eyes as the truth of what she'd done sunk in. The baby cried louder.

Nick drew in a breath, doing his best to ignore the pain. "I didn't think you had the guts."

"I told you to stop."

Wincing, he pushed himself up so that he was standing. Warm blood ran down his leg. He didn't have to look at the wound to know it was *bad*...!

D0041221

Mary Burton has published eight historical novels, two novellas and a contemporary romance novel for Intimate Moments. A graduate of Hollins University, Burton enjoys scuba diving, yoga and hiking. She is based in Richmond, Virginia, where she lives with her husband and two children.

THE TRACKER

MARY BURTON

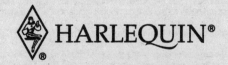

HARLEQUIN®

TORONTO • NEW YORK • LONDON
AMSTERDAM • PARIS • SYDNEY • HAMBURG
STOCKHOLM • ATHENS • TOKYO • MILAN • MADRID
PRAGUE • WARSAW • BUDAPEST • AUCKLAND

Special thanks and acknowledgment are given
to Mary Burton for her contribution
to the MONTANA MAVERICKS series.

ISBN 0-373-81120-9

THE TRACKER

This edition published by arrangement with Harlequin Books S.A.

® and TM are trademarks of the publisher. Trademarks indicated with
® are registered in the United States Patent and Trademark Office, the
Canadian Trade Marks Office and in other countries.

www.eHarlequin.com

Printed in U.S.A.

PROLOGUE

SOLDIER. Bounty hunter. Killer.

Nick Baron had been called them all.

A cold spring breeze blew as Nick strode down the main street of Thunder Canyon. His black duster grazed the top of scuffed boots and his spurs jangled as he crossed the muddy street toward the saloon.

He knew people watched him.

His gaze was hooded by his wide-brimmed hat, but he noticed the two men in front of the mercantile. They'd been deep in conversation when one had glanced up and spotted Nick heading toward them. The man's face paled. He whispered something to his companion and the two scurried across the street. A portly woman closed the curtains of her millinery shop as Nick passed. Several women hustled their children inside.

When he'd first moved west, his disregard for danger had been so complete that many outlaws had figured he'd had a death wish. In truth, he'd had nothing to lose. His bold, sometimes reckless actions had earned him a powerful reputation among those he hunted. And he'd let the rumors of his captures and the exaggerated claims of his kills grow. His ability to intimidate the roughest men had been part of the reason he'd captured so many outlaws.

Yet in the past year, he'd come to realize it wasn't just the outlaws who feared him. Decent folks, like the ones here in Thunder Canyon, were just as scared. He'd gone a long way to cleaning up this territory, and yet he was an outsider.

The realization made him bone weary. The path he'd embraced more than a decade ago now squeezed the life out of him.

Nick pushed through the doors of the saloon. At the noon hour, the place was all but deserted. The piano was silent. A reed-thin bartender wearing a stained apron wiped off a table while three miners sat by the window playing cards. The room smelled of whiskey and stale smoke.

Nick's spurs jangled as he moved across the dirt floor to a dark corner where a solitary man sat.

Sheriff Bobby Pool was well past sixty. He wore his long gray hair tied at the nape of his neck with rawhide. Thick eyebrows hovered over sharp gray eyes. A U.S. Marshal's silver star adorned the front of his jacket.

Bobby wasn't a big man—he was midsize at

best—but when Nick looked the sheriff in the eye, he'd have sworn the sheriff topped six foot, like himself. Honest, hardworking and ruthless, Sheriff Pool had become a legend in this part of Montana.

Ten years ago, Nick had met Bobby in Jackson in the Wyoming Territory. Bobby had heard three outlaws planned to storm Nick's camp at midnight and he'd warned him. The tip had saved Nick's life and Bobby had become as close a friend as Nick had ever had.

Bobby's eyes sparkled with youthful excitement as he rose and extended his hand to Nick. "Well, you look like Lucifer himself."

Nick accepted his hand. "You would, too, if you'd been in a saddle for twenty-one days straight."

Nick and the older man took a seat at the table. Both sat with their backs to the wall. Nick set his black Stetson on the table.

"You created quite a stir this morning when you turned over John Ramsey to the sheriff," Bobby said.

"So it seems."

John Ramsey had been wanted for killing a homesteader and his family. Only one member of the family—a six-year-old girl—had survived the attack by hiding in the kindling box. Ramsey had eluded the law for two years until Nick had gotten on his trail.

"Ramsey has a talent for hiding under the smallest rock. Took three weeks to find him."

Bobby rubbed his gnarled hands together. The arthritis pained him most in the spring. "He as mean as they say?"

"Just about."

Bobby absorbed the information. "So, other than smelling like a dead buffalo, how the devil are you, Nick?"

"I'd be soaking in the barber's tub right now if I hadn't gotten word you wanted to see me. I hope whatever news you have is worth keeping me from my bath."

Bobby ignored Nick's rough tone. "It's worth it."

Nick would have shot back another remark but he noticed then that Bobby looked more fatigued than normal. And Bobby wasn't one to chitchat. He'd called this meeting for a reason.

The bartender eased over to their table and glanced nervously at Nick. His hands trembled as he set down a glass and bottle of whiskey in front of Bobby. "Can I get you anything, Mr. Baron?"

"Steak and potatoes."

"Anything to wash it down? A tumbler so you can share the marshal's whiskey?"

"Just coffee."

"Yes, sir." The bartender hurried into the back room as if he were happy for the task.

Bobby's walrus mustache twitched when he laughed. "You still got the knack."

Nick leaned back in his chair and crossed his legs at his ankles. "Knack?"

"To make people jump. I ain't seen a bounty hunter who could strike fear in a man's heart like you."

Irritation rose inside him. "Part of the job, I suppose."

Bobby filled his whiskey glass. "You sound like you're not happy about it."

He rarely shared his thoughts, but when he did, it was only to Bobby. "Until recently, I welcomed the fear. It made the job easier."

Bobby's chair creaked as he leaned forward. "And no more?"

"I'm tired of the travel. I'm tired of waking up and not knowing what town I'm in or if there is a shooter behind a bush or building waiting to put a bullet in my back."

Bobby nodded. "Been there myself. Maybe you should retire. I'm planning to."

A ghost of a smile touched Nick's lips. "You have been saying that for three years. Last I heard you *had* retired."

"I know. Seemed there was too much work. But I

aim to walk away from law enforcement this summer."

"I can't imagine you sitting on a rocker."

"Can't say I'm ready for the chair," Bobby said, grinning. "But I bought myself a plot of land outside of Thunder Canyon. I aim to raise horses."

The news took Nick by surprise. "I wouldn't have believed it if you hadn't told me yourself."

His chest puffed with pride. "Well, it's a done deal."

Nick sighed. "I've been thinking about settling down a lot lately. I'm tired of being alone."

Bobby raised an eyebrow. "*You're* tired of being alone?"

"You make it sound as if I have a disease."

"You're making money hand over fist. Hell, Ramsey had to be worth almost a grand."

Nick sighed. "How much money can a man spend in a lifetime?"

"Don't know. But I *do* know that living without money can be a real pain. A marshal's pay is miserably low."

The bartender returned to the table with a clean mug and a pot of freshly brewed coffee. "You still take it black?"

Nick nodded his thanks. "That's right."

The bartender started to back away. "Your meal will be right up."

"Appreciate it," Nick said. He poured himself a cup of coffee and waited until the bartender was out of earshot. "In the last year, I've disliked the long weeks on the trail. I'm losing my edge."

"Somehow I can't picture you losing your edge *or* living around people."

There'd been a time long ago when Nick had been surrounded by family and friends. He'd looked forward to holiday furloughs filled with lively music, parties and laughter. "I just might surprise you. I've started to think to the future, slowing down, building a spread where I can raise horses." He sipped his coffee. "Hell, I've even dreamed of a wife and children."

Bobby's eyes darkened with approval. "No more running from the past."

Nick didn't argue with the statement. The old man knew Nick's wife, Crystal, had died in Virginia giving birth to a child sired while Nick had been stationed at an army post in Kansas. The baby's father had turned out to be Nick's brother, Gregory. Nick had nearly beaten Gregory to death when he'd found out. Though acquitted of any crime, Nick had left Virginia and never returned.

Bobby's demeanor turned serious. He downed half his glass of whiskey. For a moment he was silent. "As a man gets older, he starts to think about the things he's left unsaid."

Nick's gaze sharpened. "You sound like a man who's ready to die."

"I have no plans to die anytime soon. It's just that…well, you've been a good friend to me. Hell, you're more like a son than a friend."

Nick's throat tightened. He wasn't comfortable with emotion. Feelings were best buried and forgotten. "What's your point, old man?"

"You could go in on the ranch with me. I could use a partner like you," Bobby said.

Surprisingly, the offer tempted him. "Be careful, I just might take you up on it."

Bobby traced the rim of his whiskey glass. "I never make an offer unless I'm serious."

For the first time in a good while, excitement sparked in Nick. "Tell me about this land of yours."

Bobby leaned forward, his eyes bright. "Dandy bit of acreage about two days' ride west of the canyon's mouth. Got a stream running through it. Lots of land for horses. Plenty of room for two cabins, if you can actually find a woman to tolerate you."

"I'd like to take a look at it."

"You mean that?"

"Yep."

Bobby leaned back in his chair, a satisfied smile on his face. "I can just see the sign now. Pool and Baron."

"Or better, Baron and Pool."

The old man's grin widened. "You think you can settle down? As much as you say you hate the travel, do you really think you'd be content to put down roots?"

"Only way to find out is to try."

The marshal nodded. "The bounty hunting will always be there if you change your mind."

The truth of his words made Nick both sad and angry. "That's one thing I've learned in the last ten years. There will always be outlaws."

The bartender delivered Nick's steak and retreated. Charred on the outside and raw in the center, it was just like a thousand other steaks he'd eaten over the last decade. He took one bite and chewed. It tasted the same as it always did, yet he'd lost his taste for it. He set his knife and fork down and pushed the plate away.

Nick noticed then that Bobby had drunk only half his whiskey. Before Bobby went on a marshaling job, he always left his whiskey glass unfinished, promising to drain the remainder when he returned. He should have known Bobby couldn't walk away from the work. "You have a job."

"You know me too well."

"Who are you after this time?"

He leaned closer to Nick and lowered his voice.

"I'm providing security for the railroad's payroll. Twenty thousand dollars in gold."

Nick whistled. "A lot of money."

"Damn stupid, if you ask me. Only a fool would move that much money at one time. Just inviting trouble. But the railroad brass isn't interested in my opinion. They just want my gun."

"This a marshaling job?"

"Nope." He pulled off his badge and laid it on the table. "The money the railroad is paying will cover the cost of my breeding stock. I telegraphed Butte this morning and retired from law enforcement."

"You want me to ride along?"

"Nah. We've got twelve men guarding the train car. Got enough ammunition between us to blow any outlaw to kingdom come."

Nick smiled, but worry nibbled at his gut. He picked up the tarnished star. "So this is your last job?"

Bobby drew an imaginary X over his heart. "On my mother's grave, I swear that this is it. Fact, why don't you keep that star as a souvenir of the old days?"

"I'll return it when you get back."

NICK NEVER GAVE Bobby back his star.

Their dreams of building a ranch vanished three

days later, when word arrived that the train carrying the gold had been robbed by two masked gunmen. Five of the twelve men guarding the train had been killed, the other seven badly wounded.

Bobby was among the dead.

Nick brought Bobby's body back to Thunder Canyon and saw it properly buried.

Then, at sunrise of the next day, Nick began his hunt for the killers.

CHAPTER ONE

Butte, Montana
June 1883

NICK STOOD in the shadows staring at the Silver Slipper brothel. The sun had set and the sky had settled into that hazy blue of twilight. He leaned against the wall of the hardware store and stared at the second-story window.

He had called in every favor in his search for any lead that would help him track the outlaws who had murdered Bobby.

It had taken three months, but he'd finally found out that Frank Palmer and his brother Monty were responsible for the railroad gold robbery and Bobby's killing.

Nick discovered that the railroad theft was their biggest job to date. Until last year, the Palmer brothers had specialized in petty crimes—robbing miners, general stores and the occasional homestead. All small scale.

Things had changed eighteen months ago, when Monty had met Jade Fletcher in the Silver Slipper whorehouse. He'd fallen in love with the house's most popular sporting girl. Soon after their marriage, Monty had started robbing banks with his brother. Clearly, Jade was doing the thinking. Likely, she had masterminded the gold robbery that got Bobby killed.

The bounty on the Palmer boys and the missing gold was the highest Nick had ever seen offered— one thousand dollars. But he didn't care about the money. This job was about justice for his friend. Nick wouldn't rest until he saw Frank and Monty Palmer swing.

Nick had nearly caught up with Frank and Monty last month near Bozeman, but he'd lost their trail in a late May snowstorm. A week ago he'd gotten word that Monty and Jade were headed toward Butte. When Nick arrived in town, he'd quickly learned that Jade and Monty were staying at the Sliver Slipper brothel.

He thought it odd they'd returned to the brothel where Jade had worked. They'd made a sloppy mistake, but Nick wasn't complaining. He took every break he could get.

Nick stared up at Jade and Monty's room. Piano music drifted from the building.

The shadow of a slender woman passed in front

of the second-story window. He'd never seen Jade in person, but he'd heard she was a statuesque woman with coal-black hair. The unidentified woman in Jade's room was petite.

However, an anonymous sporting girl didn't matter. Monty and Jade did. Soon, Frank would show— he was never far behind Monty and Jade. And when Frank arrived, Nick would have them all.

Soon, it would be over.

ELLIE CROSSED the small room to the threshold where Miss Adeline, madam of the Silver Slipper, hovered. The woman's bright red lipstick matched her silk dress. The vibrant color made her pale skin look gaunt.

"The baby is fine, but the mother is dying," Ellie said.

Miss Adeline frowned, unwilling to enter the room thick with the scent of birthing. She refused to look at the pale woman lying in the bed or the swaddled baby nestled next to her. Music and laughter from the first-floor saloon echoed below them.

"Are you sure there's nothing you can do for Jade?" Miss Adeline asked.

Ellie's back ached and her head pounded with fatigue. "She's lost too much blood. I've tried to stop the bleeding, but nothing has worked."

The lines feathering the corners of Miss Adeline's

painted eyes deepened. "She was so healthy and strong. She was laughing this morning and asking for fried eggs."

Ellie had seen births go wrong before. Every time it was heartbreaking. "I wish there was something else I could do."

Gold bracelets jangled on Miss Adeline's thin wrist as she rubbed her forehead. "Monty's not going to be happy. He trusted me to take care of Jade. The man depends on her."

"Where is he? I sent for him over an hour ago." Ellie couldn't soften the anger in her voice. She'd grown up around men like Monty Palmer.

Miss Adeline's gown shimmered in the lantern light. "He's down the hallway with one of the girls. He said he was tense and needed to relax."

A tart remark sprang to mind but Ellie kept silent. Miss Adeline dealt with any kind of rebellion harshly. "Jade doesn't have much time left. You may want to interrupt him. If there are any last words to be said, they'd best be spoken now. I doubt Jade will live through the hour."

Miss Adeline nodded. "This is the last thing I needed today. The way my luck's running, Monty will shoot up the place when he finds out and I'll never see my share of the gold."

"What gold?"

"Never mind," Miss Adeline snapped. She started from the room and then stopped. "Is the child a boy or girl?"

"A girl."

She sighed. "Monty's not going to like that, either. He's been talking about having a boy—Monty Junior is what he was going to call him." She left, her full silk skirts swishing as she moved down the carpeted hallway.

Ellie closed the door, shutting out the noise and the smell of whiskey and tobacco. Lantern light flickered on the lilac-colored wallpaper. With a heavy heart, she faced the bed. Jade's face was deathly pale. Her long black hair fanned out on the white pillow.

"Ellie," Jade whispered.

Ellie sat on the small stool beside the bed. She leaned over and checked the baby, who lay sleeping next to her mother. "Shh, you must rest."

Her eyes opened. "Where is the baby?"

"Right beside you." She brushed the damp hair off Jade's face. She and Jade had never been friends while Jade had lived in this house.

Jade didn't have the strength to lift her head. "I can't see her face."

Ellie picked up the baby and, folding back the quilted blanket, held her up so that Jade could see her face. "She's a beauty."

"Is she all right?"

"Yes. A fine set of lungs. She's got all her fingers and toes, and your black hair." Ellie tried to keep her voice light.

A faint smile curled the edges of Jade's lips. "As long as she doesn't have her father's nose."

Ellie's throat tightened. It frustrated her she couldn't do more. "Have you thought of a name for her?"

"Rose. It was my grandmother's name."

The baby stirred and yawned, unmindful of the turmoil around her. "The name suits her. She looks like a little rosebud."

Tears pooled in Jade's eyes. A tear trickled down her hollow cheek. Two years ago she'd been surrounded by men and laughing as if she were holding court like a queen. "She's the best thing that ever happened to me."

"You did real well, Jade."

Another tear rolled down Jade's cheek. "I can't believe the Lord blessed me with such a beautiful baby. I've done a lot of bad things, Ellie. I don't deserve such a precious child."

"You shouldn't worry about the past, Jade. None of that matters now. You need to get strong so you can take care of Rose."

Jade swallowed. "I'm dying, aren't I?"

As ever, Jade was sharp as a bowie knife. Fooling her was next to impossible. "You're very tired and need rest."

Jade met her gaze. Her watery blue eyes possessed an intensity that shook Ellie. "Ellie, please don't lie to me now."

Unshed tears burned in Ellie's eyes. She hesitated, unsure her voice would be steady when she spoke. "Yes," she said, her voice a hoarse whisper. "You're dying."

Jade closed her eyes and a heavy silence settled between them. For a moment Ellie thought that Jade had slipped into unconsciousness.

"Take care of Rose for me," Jade said weakly.

"Of course I will."

Jade lifted her hand and grabbed Ellie's wrist. She squeezed. Her grip had surprising strength. "I mean *forever*, Ellie. Don't give her to Monty or Adeline. He doesn't want a daughter. And Adeline will turn her over to an orphanage or sell her."

Ellie didn't argue with Jade's assessment. "Jade, I don't know anything about children. I've lived my whole life above this whorehouse."

Jade moistened her full, pale lips. "You've always had a good heart and you do what's right. Rose wouldn't have survived the birthing if not for you. You're the kind of mother my girl needs."

Ellie stared down at the baby. The thought of raising a child was overwhelming. Bottles. Blankets. Clothes. Diapers. She didn't know where to start. Lord, and what about milk? "Don't you have any other family to take the baby?"

"They cut me off a long time ago. And even if they hadn't, I wouldn't give Rose to them. She deserves better." Jade's hand fell back to the mattress. "Rose will be all alone without you. There'll be no one to keep her safe."

A protective urge welled up in Ellie. Her own mother had died when she was six. Adeline had allowed Ellie to stay, but there'd been no one to love or to care for her when she was sick or afraid. It was a childhood she'd not have wished on anyone.

"Monty hasn't seen her," Ellie said. "He could fall in love with her the minute he sees her. He might not want to give up his flesh and blood."

She shook her head. The slight movement seemed to be almost too much for her. "He won't. Having the baby was my idea, not his. He couldn't care less about a child, especially a girl."

Ellie clutched the tiny infant. She pictured the child, alone and crying, desperate for someone to pick her up.

The child started to move her mouth around Ellie's breast, searching for her nipple. A strong maternal instinct swept over Ellie. She'd delivered this child into the world. She'd been the first to hold her. Hers had been the first face the baby had seen. She wanted Rose safe and loved.

But how could she raise a baby?

"*Swear* you'll keep her." Jade's voice was a faint whisper now.

Ellie had no business making such a promise to Jade. And yet she heard herself saying, "I swear."

Jade smiled. "You won't regret it."

Ellie stared into the baby's face. The child had stopped her rooting and fallen asleep. "No, I won't regret it."

"There is a Bible by the bed on the table. Do you see it?" Jade said.

She picked up the pocket-size book. "Yes."

"It's all I got for Rose. It belonged to my grandmother. I carry it with me always. Keep it safe and close to you. It's worth more than you can imagine."

"I will."

"When Rose is old enough, give it to her. Tell her I loved her."

Ellie tucked the Bible into her apron pocket. "I will tell her, Jade."

Jade's next words died on her lips. Her eyes closed. Within seconds her breathing grew shallow as the life drained from her body. And then her breathing stopped.

For a long moment Ellie cradled the baby, over-whelmed by the sudden turn her life had taken. The noise from the saloon seeped through the floor-boards. She'd never been around children, not even when she was a child. Her whole life had been spent serving drinks, cooking meals and cleaning up after drunken customers. Lord, what was she going to do?

She'd saved just about every penny she'd earned, but it wasn't much. And where would she go? Every-one in Butte knew she worked at the Silver Slipper and no one would give her a decent job. She'd have to leave town—start over somewhere else.

The music from the floor below stopped. The sud-den silence caught her attention. She stood and moved to the door, listening.

"Where are Monty and Jade?" The loud voice came from downstairs. Ellie recognized it instantly. It was Frank Palmer, Monty's brother.

Frank scared her far more than Monty did. The outlaw had been visiting the house for five years. He'd never bought a woman when he came. Instead he'd just sat in her kitchen, eating his meal, silently watching her.

Her heart thrumming, Ellie held the baby close and moved out into the hallway.

From the upstairs landing, she saw Frank at the foot of the stairs. He had a long scraggly beard and shoulder-length hair. He wasn't very tall, but his upper body was thick and muscular. His clothes were coated in a month's worth of trail dust and several of the girls moved away from him as if he smelled bad.

"Where's Monty?" Frank shouted. "His brother wants him!"

Ellie tightened her hold on the baby. The girls had whispered that Frank, Monty and Jade had robbed the railroad. She'd been too busy with the birthing to listen, but now she wished she knew more.

Miss Adeline scurried out of her backroom office, a tumbler of whiskey in her hand. Shock registered on her face when she saw Frank Palmer before she plastered on her trademark smile. "Frank!"

"Where's Monty?" he demanded.

"Upstairs with Kelly."

"Monty!" he shouted.

Frank's arrival couldn't be good. Ellie moved to the door leading to the back staircase and opened it. Lingering on the top step, she stood ready to dash downstairs if need be.

Monty stumbled out of a room, fastening his pants. His face was a mirror copy of his brother's. The only difference was that he stood several inches taller. Behind him, Kelly, dressed only in a chemise, strolled out. She took one look at Frank, backed into the room and slammed the door.

"Frank?" Monty said, panic in his voice. "How'd you find me?"

Frank drew his gun and started toward the stairs. "I want my gold back."

Monty glanced around, as if looking for a place to hide. He shoved a trembling hand through his thick black hair. "I don't have your gold, Frank. Jade's the one that hid it. She got mad a few weeks ago when she caught me with a whore. While I was sleeping off a drunk, she stashed it somewhere. Don't worry, once she cooled off, I was gonna talk to her. You know how I can sweet-talk her."

"I'm tired of your talk, Monty. When you picked Jade over me, you saw to it that things would never be the same between us." Without warning, he shot Monty in the heart. The man dropped to the floor dead.

Ellie jumped.

The girls screamed.

Miss Adeline swayed, pressing her hand into her stomach.

Casually, Frank replaced his gun in its holster. "Now, which room is Jade's?"

Miss Adeline struggled to keep her expression calm. "Last door on the right."

"Time ol' Mrs. Palmer and Frank had a chat about *my* gold."

Ellie pressed her back against the stairwell wall, her heart thundering in her chest. Frank would soon find out that Jade was dead. And then he'd start to ask questions. He'd want to know who was with her when she'd died. Miss Adeline wouldn't hesitate to tell him Ellie was the one he wanted.

In that split second, Ellie decided to run.

She started down the back staircase, no longer questioning the fact that she and the baby had to leave the Silver Slipper and Butte for good. They'd have to disappear if they wanted to live.

Nerves nearly made her trip when she reached the last step. She caught herself on the railing with one hand, clutching the baby with the other. Quickly, she laid the baby in a large, shallow basket she used for shopping and bolted out the back door.

The night air was warm. A sliver of moon dangled in the black evening sky. Clouds drifted from the west. The scent of rain was heavy.

Ellie thought of the horses Miss Adeline kept at the livery. She could take one and be gone before anyone thought to look for her outside of the brothel.

She started to run. She'd taken just five steps when she ran into a wall of hard muscle. She'd have fallen backward if strong arms hadn't captured her forearms and steadied her. It felt as if cold steel banded her arms. Naked fear nearly stopped her heart.

"Who fired those shots inside?" The cold, menacing voice had her lifting her gaze.

Dark eyes stared down at her from under a low-crowned black hat. The man's rawboned face was all hard planes and angles. Several days' growth of beard covered his square jaw. His nose looked as if it had been broken before.

She pulled back, a small choking sound in her throat. She couldn't find it in her to speak.

The stranger tightened his long fingers on her arms. He gave her a small shake to snap her out of her fear. *"Who got shot?"*

"Frank Palmer shot his brother Monty," Ellie blurted, hoping he didn't hear the terror in her voice.

"Dead?"

"Yes."

"Anybody else come in with Frank?"

"Anyone else?" Her confused mind wouldn't work.

"Other *outlaws*."

"No."

He hesitated, as if considering what she'd said.

"Would you let loose of me? I don't know anything else."

The sound of her voice seemed to bring him back from his thoughts. "Why are you running?"

With the darkness around them, it seemed they were the only two people in the world. They stood inches apart and she could feel his hot breath on her skin. The baby in the basket was wedged between them.

"I'm not," she lied.

His face hardened in the dim moonlight. He leaned closer to her so that his nose was only inches from hers. "I can smell the fear on you. You're running from something, girl."

She glanced toward the back door of the Silver Slipper, wishing she could run inside and lock the door. But she couldn't go back. "Miss Adeline asked me to run an errand."

"Did she?"

She tried to pull her arms from his grip. She might as well have been trying to break iron. "I really must hurry. She's not a woman to be disobeyed."

"But you are defying her, aren't you?" His voice was as hard as granite.

She stopped her squirming, amazed he could peer into her brain and read her thoughts. Tonight she was breaking most all of Adeline's rules. There'd be hell to pay if she got caught.

Rose squawked.

The stranger dropped his gaze to the basket. He flicked the blanket aside with his finger. Rose, still sleeping, yawned.

Without warning, he stepped back. "You better run fast, girl. All hell's about to break lose."

Ellie didn't need to be told twice.

CHAPTER TWO

Spring Rock Coach Station
August 1883

"AND IF ANYONE looks at you cross-eyed, shoot 'em!" Annie Bennett said. Annie had hired Ellie almost two months ago as a cook at the Spring Rock stop, a place she'd run for almost twenty years. The two had become close friends in a short time and had learned to rely on each other.

Ellie nodded. "I will."

Annie checked the cinch on her mare's saddle. She had tied back her blond hair and donned a floppy hat, pants and a range coat. She reminded Ellie of a wiry cowhand, not a petite, slender woman who under all that gear looked much younger than her forty-five years. "I should be gone about three weeks." Annie made an annual trek to the mountains to visit her mother and father, to make sure they were well before the snows came. "I worry that they're getting too old to manage the place."

"If what you told me about them is true, I suspect they will be fine."

During the last couple of months, Ellie had enjoyed the stories of Annie's childhood. Annie's mother, Charity, had been married to a missionary when she'd moved to Thunder Canyon. Indians had attacked their caravan and everyone in the mission party had been killed except Charity, who was pregnant with Annie. Black Sun, an Arapaho warrior, had saved Charity and delivered Annie. Charity and Black Sun had fallen in love. Black Sun had adopted Annie and loved her as much as his sons.

Annie pulled leather gloves from her pocket and tugged them on. "You've got enough provisions for two months. But if something should happen and you need more, ride into town. I've an account at Douglas's mercantile."

"Rose and I will be fine," Ellie said, careful to keep any hint of worry out of her voice.

Ellie had never spent a night at the coach stop alone. The idea didn't sit well with her, but she'd never tell Annie that. She didn't like the woman worrying over her when she had such a trip to make.

"Annie, we need to get on the road now," said Mike McKinney, striding out of the barn.

Mike was a tall, burly man with a full beard and broad shoulders. In his mid-thirties, he was a driver for the Starlight Express. He'd done so well, his boss, Holden McGowan, had given him the northern routes. This last year, he had visited the Spring Rock station often. In the last two months, he'd been by almost weekly.

"I know," Annie said gruffly.

"If we don't leave now, we won't make the foothills by dark," he said.

Despite the irritation in her voice, Annie's blue eyes softened when she looked at Mike. He and Annie both said they were friends, but Ellie had quickly recognized that they were in love.

Mike had arrived at the stop yesterday on his regular run. When Annie told him she was heading north to see her family, he'd insisted on riding with her. Annie had agreed without an argument. Ellie suspected Mike was going to ask Black Sun for Annie's hand in marriage.

"I'm ready to go," Annie said.

Mike cocked an eyebrow. "Is that the fourth or fifth time she's said that?"

Ellie laughed. "Sixth."

He laughed. "Ellie, the horses are set and you shouldn't have to fuss with them until sunset."

"I know what to do," Ellie said. Annie had showed her how to care for the six horses her first week here.

"Take care of that baby," Annie said, hugging Ellie.

"And keep the shotgun close," Mike said, preparing to climb up into his saddle.

Ellie had been at her wits' end when she and Rose had arrived at Annie's stop two months ago. Ellie hadn't eaten in two days and she'd spent all her savings on canned milk she'd purchased from a wagon train.

Annie hadn't asked any questions when Ellie had claimed to be a widow. Nor had she said a word when Ellie had pulled out the bottle at the dinner table. The next morning, there'd been a pitcher of freshly boiled milk and Rose's bottle had been cleaned. Annie had offered Ellie a job that day. Ellie had accepted.

"It's late in the season, so you won't see too many customers," Annie said. "Maybe a few miners. There'll still be fools who haven't gotten word the mines are almost played out."

Annie had told all this to Ellie four or five times.

"Go!" Ellie said, shooing them away. "At the rate you two are moving, it'll be snowing before you leave."

The three laughed. Annie and Mike mounted their horses and reined them around toward the stage road that threaded toward the distant mountains. Ellie watched Mike and Annie ride off until they vanished into the horizon.

She turned back toward the cabin. Except for the gentle whisper of the wind in the trees, there was nothing but silence.

Ellie folded her arms over her chest. The silence could be louder than the drunks in the brothel and at times just as unnerving. A deep loneliness settled inside her. Except for the two weeks when she'd traveled from Butte to the coach stop, she'd never really been alone before. And the truth was, it didn't sit well.

But Rose was thriving in the fresh country air, and they were far away from Butte and Frank Palmer. A little quiet was a small price to pay.

Ellie headed toward Annie's two-story stone building. A wooden front porch roped along three sides of the first floor. Black shutters flanked the glass-paned windows. The place was simple, practical to a fault, but there was an inviting air about it.

Ellie climbed the three front steps and moved inside the coach stop. The first floor was divided into three rooms. A great room on the east side dominated most of the space. This room was the heart of the stop, housing the large dining area and the kitchen. The dining area was simply furnished with an oversize eating table surrounded by eight rope-bottomed chairs. Twin rockers sat in front of a tall stone hearth. The kitchen had a large black stove, worktable and ample wood counter.

Across from the great room were two other rooms. The one in the back of the house was a large storage room. The second, located near the front door, had also been a storage room once. Though Annie had offered Ellie a room upstairs, she'd always preferred to sleep as far from customers as possible. Annie had allowed Ellie to clean the storeroom out and turn it into a bedroom for her and Rose.

The upstairs housed Annie's room, along with three guest rooms for overnight visitors.

The smell of rabbit stew and fresh bread filled the cabin as Ellie went inside and peeked into her room, where a quilt-lined cradle sat by her bed. Baby Rose slept on her back in the cradle, her little lips pursed into a frown. Ellie smiled, her heart warming as she stared at the child.

Annie had produced the cradle from the attic when Ellie had first arrived. Later, Mike had told Ellie that Annie had lost her first husband, the original coach stop owner, and a daughter more than twenty years ago. She'd lived here alone since then.

Emotion tightened Ellie's throat. She didn't know what she'd do if she lost Rose. She touched the baby's cheek. In her heart, the child was hers completely now. "I'll never leave you, baby girl, never."

Being this close to Rose soothed any worries Ellie

had about spending the next few weeks alone. They had made it this far.

"There's no sense worrying," she whispered, hugging her arms around her chest.

She and Rose were far from Butte and Frank Palmer.

No one was going to find her out here.

They were safe.

IT WAS PAST NOON when Nick Baron reached the hill overlooking the Spring Rock station. His gaze skimmed the two-story stone building, corral, barn, pigpen and henhouse.

He spotted the redheaded woman taking in laundry and knew he'd found the right place. The wind rustled her calico skirts around her ankles and flapped the edges of a sheet she wrestled into a fold.

For a moment he just sat and stared at her. He'd spent weeks tracking her and now he'd found her. For such a little bit of a woman, she'd been hard to find.

He watched as Ellie subdued the sheet and put it in the basket.

Nick had been a fool to let her go that night in Butte. But he'd been so sure that he had Frank, Monty and Jade Palmer and he'd seen no reason to entangle a young woman and a baby in his fight.

But the precious seconds he'd hesitated with Ellie

had been all it had taken for Frank to slip away. He'd questioned Adeline about Jade and Monty and learned that Ellie, a Silver Slipper sporting girl, had disappeared with Jade's baby. Adeline had grumbled that Ellie was a greedy, ungrateful girl who'd likely learned of the gold from Jade and had run away so she could get it for herself.

Nick had set out after Frank but heavy rains had washed away the outlaw's tracks and Nick had lost his trail. He'd searched for Frank for more than a month before he'd given up and directed his sights on Ellie.

Ellie picked up her laundry basket and headed inside the house.

If Frank were smart, he'd head north to Canada or south to Mexico, but Nick suspected he'd do neither. He'd not leave Montana without his gold, even though every lawman and bounty hunter in the region was looking for him. Soon, he'd figure out Ellie had been the last to see Jade and he'd come after her.

Nick didn't like the idea of using Ellie to get Frank, but there seemed no way around it now. She was his only link to the outlaw now. And until Frank was captured, her life was in danger.

He kicked his heels into the sides of his horse and rode across the flat land.

He leaned forward in his saddle. "Ellie Watson!"

The redhead appeared at the door. She gripped a

shotgun in her small hands. Her eyes were as wide as saucers, her skin moon-pale and her hair a bit wild, as if the topknot couldn't quite hold it. "What can I do for you, mister?"

Ellie was just as he remembered. She wasn't a great beauty, but her froth of red curls and moss-green eyes gave her a freshness uncommon to sporting girls. Something about her made him think of afternoons spent naked in a feather bed.

"I've been looking for you for several weeks," he said.

She stiffened. "I don't see why."

He climbed down off his horse, but he didn't approach her. A skittish woman with a loaded gun was nothing to be trifled with. He pulled off his hat so she could see his face clearly. "We met at the Silver Slipper two months ago."

She lifted her chin a fraction. The color drained from her cheeks. "I don't know you."

"Yes, you do."

He could almost hear her mind working. She was wondering if she could make it to that barn behind him and reach one of the horses. She rightly figured she couldn't. "What do you want?"

"I want Frank Palmer."

A panicked look settled in her eyes. "I don't know any Frank Palmer."

"I spoke with Adeline." He dropped the horse's reins and took one step toward her. "Adeline said that you were the last person to see Jade alive. She also said Frank knows that, too."

"There were a lot of people in and out of her room toward the end." Her voice was tight and tense.

She was a bad liar. "I've come to find out what Jade told you about the stolen gold."

Her brow knotted. She seemed genuinely confused by his comment. "Jade never said a word to me about gold."

She was afraid, but he was willing to be patient. If they stood here long enough, he knew she'd slip up or he could rush her and snatch the gun from her hands. "I know you delivered her baby. It's understandable that two women who shared what you two did would have a bond."

"I don't know—" A cry drifted out of the cabin. Ellie glanced over her shoulder and then met his gaze again.

"I see you kept the child," he said. Admiration washed over him. It couldn't have been easy to travel the rough country between here and Butte with a baby.

She was silent and he thought she'd not answer him until she finally said, "Jade gave me the baby to raise, but she never said anything about gold."

He sighed. "That's not the kind of secret Jade would take to her grave."

"She didn't plan on dying so quick."

"Ellie, you better think real hard about that gold. Unless I take it off your hands, Frank will. And I can guarantee that he won't be as polite as me. Be grateful that I found you before Frank did."

Her eyes narrowed. "How do you know Frank?"

"He and I have business."

Her gaze flicked over him. He knew he looked rough. "I want no part of whatever *business* you and Frank are about. I want to be left in peace."

"Like it or not, you are part of it. So is that baby."

"She's *my* baby."

"Jade birthed her."

Her face tightened. "Leave me alone."

He took several steps toward her. His spurs jingled with each step. "I won't hurt you or the baby, Ellie. But I need that gold. Give it to me before Frank comes looking for it."

She took a step back. With trembling hands she raised the double-barreled shotgun. "Don't come a step closer, mister."

If he sprang forward, he would have a good chance of getting the gun. "I'm not leaving here without the gold, Ellie."

She lifted her gun a fraction higher. "One more step and I'll shoot."

He hesitated. "You don't have it in you."

"Try me."

Her tone, more than her words, had his eyes narrowing. "That gun's old," he said.

"And very well oiled."

"You've got grit, girl. But I've been riding hard for weeks now and I'm in no mood for games."

She swallowed.

"If you shoot me, there'll be no one here to protect you from Frank."

Her eyes narrowed. "For all I know, *you* are working with Frank. And I'm not here alone. I've got friends."

He lifted an eyebrow. "Where are they?"

"Close."

He laughed, but the sound held no joy. His gaze still on her, he held up his hands as if in surrender. "I don't want trouble."

Ellie's gaze dropped to the six-shooter at his side. She gripped the barrel so tight her knuckles turned white. "I don't want to kill you. Just leave me be and let me return to my life."

"Can't do that." He took another step and then another.

She squeezed the trigger.

Nick reacted quickly, diving to his left. He'd hoped he'd be quick enough to get out of the way of the gun, but he wasn't.

Buckshot splayed out of the barrel, striking him in the right leg. Blinding pain seared through his thigh as the acrid smell of smoke filled his nostrils. He hit the ground hard.

Ellie screamed. She stood on the porch, frozen, her hands still locked around the gun. Tears welled in her eyes as the truth of what she'd done sank in. The baby cried louder.

Nick sucked in a breath, doing his best to ignore the blinding pain. "I didn't think you had the guts."

"I told you to stop."

Wincing, he pushed himself up so that he was standing. Warm blood ran down his leg. He didn't have to look at the wound to know it was bad.

Upset, she lowered her gun.

He took the opportunity and lunged at her like a wounded bear. He grabbed the gun and jerked it out of her hand. He gripped her arm.

She tried to twist free. "Let go of me."

He could smell the coppery scent of his blood. He'd taken down men twice his size and meaner than Satan. Yet here he stood, likely bleeding to death, shot by a little bit of a woman.

"You should have *listened* to me," she wailed.

"Thanks to you, it doesn't look like I'm going anywhere." His pant leg was wet with blood.

The baby's cries echoed in his skull. He felt dizzy.

Soon his wound would get the better of him. Soon he'd pass out.

His gaze dropped to hers. She was all that stood between him and death. A man could do all the planning he wanted but the truth was, plans were fragile. People who were quick to respond to change were the ones who survived.

"If I die, you hang," he lied. He regretted the raw fear in her eyes but there was no avoiding it. He needed her help.

Ellie lifted her chin. "Who would care if I killed an outlaw? I'll likely collect a reward."

A tense smile curved the edges of his lips. "Lady, I'm no outlaw."

She twisted her hands. "Of course you are."

He reached inside his vest pocket and pulled out the silver star that had belonged to Bobby Pool. He'd carried the star as a tribute to his friend. Now he prayed it would convince Ellie to save his life.

Nick handed the star to Ellie before he dropped to his knees.

She held it in her small hand. Her face contracted. She looked as though she was going to faint.

CHAPTER THREE

ELLIE HAD SHOT a marshal!

Her head spun. She could feel a hangman's noose sliding around her neck.

"You should have said *something!* If I had known you were a marshal, I wouldn't have shot you."

He grimaced. "I'll remember that next time."

She knelt beside him. Her hands trembled. "I thought marshals were supposed to wear their stars on their lapels? The sheriff in Butte *always* wears his star on his coat."

The marshal met her gaze. "Ellie, do we really have to go into this right now? I'm bleeding." His voice was calm, as if they were sitting in church on Sunday.

Ellie swallowed her panic and glanced down at his leg. "No, no. Of course not." She reached for the torn fabric of his pant leg, ready to rip it free so she could get a better look at the wound.

The marshal grabbed her wrist. "You know anything about bullet wounds?"

Her skin tingled where he touched her. "Yes." She'd seen her share at the Silver Slipper. "Let's get you to bed." She wrapped her arms around his shoulders and helped him up. He kept the bulk of his weight on his left leg.

He winced. "Where'd you learn about wounds?"

"Chin Lo, a medicine man who worked for Miss Adeline, taught me everything he knew."

"Let's hope he knew a lot."

His dry humor caught her off guard. She looked at him as if seeing him for the first time. Instead of a menacing monster, she saw a man. A very attractive man.

She refocused. "I've seen bullets dug out, wounds stitched, and I've mixed the salves."

"You ever doctored anyone alone?"

"Only once." She'd delivered Jade's baby.

"Should I ask?"

"No." Hugging him close, she guided him into the house and toward her room. He'd never make it upstairs.

His face was as pale as her petticoats, but he didn't complain as he limped inside. Gingerly she lowered him onto her mattress. The springs groaned as the mattress sagged. The baby's cries had quieted. Ellie glanced into the crib. Rose had stopped crying and her face had turned in Ellie's direction.

Ellie helped the marshal shrug off his coat and then tossed it onto the floor. A deep stain of blood spread from his right thigh up to his hip and down to his knee. "Mister, you should have stopped when I said to."

Pain deepened the sun-etched lines at the corner of his eyes. "Looks like I underestimated you," he said quietly.

"You're not the first." The man's breathing was getting shallower. She prayed he wouldn't die.

He glanced at the wound. "This is a complication I never considered."

"Tell me about it."

As gently as she could manage, she lifted his feet onto the bed. When he stretched out, his large frame barely fit the mattress. Ellie pulled off his boots and set them on the floor beside the bed.

She reached for the buckle of his gun belt.

He grabbed her hand. "No."

"It'll be hard enough cleaning the wound as it is. I'll never get to it if I got to work around a holster."

He swallowed and pulled his gun from the holster. "Take the belt."

He glanced at the crib at the foot of her bed and looked at the sleeping baby. He frowned, as if the sight of the child troubled him.

Immediately, Ellie pushed the cradle away from her bed toward the corner and away from his gaze.

"I would never hurt her," the marshal said, his voice oddly gruff.

She could feel his gaze on her as she positioned the cradle. "I don't take chances with Rose."

She hurried to the kitchen and retrieved the medical kit Annie kept over the stove and the kettle she'd only just heated for tea.

She poured hot water into the washbasin, mixed it with some cool well water and then washed her hands. Her hands cleaned and dried, she carried Annie's stash of bandages and the rest of the hot water to the bed.

The marshal laid his head back on the pillow, his face tight with pain. His body was all muscle, long and lean, sinewy but not bulky. An injured predator was twice as dangerous.

"You got a name?" she said.

"Nick Baron."

"Well, Marshal Baron, I'll make this as painless as I can for you."

He nodded.

She pulled a half-full bottle of whiskey from the medicine box. "I don't have any herbs to help you sleep, but if you drink the whiskey, it will help a little with the pain."

The marshal shook his head. "No booze."

"This is no time to be tough. It will help you relax."

"No."

"It's not going to be easy." She dreaded what was to come.

"No whiskey."

Frustrated, she set the bottle on the table. "Suit yourself. But don't say I didn't warn you."

She removed a very sharp knife from the box, submerged it in the basin of hot water and then doused the blade with whiskey. Carefully she dried the knife, aware the marshal's gaze tracked her every move.

She leaned toward him, the blade gleaming in the sunlight from the one window at the head of her bed.

Likely by reflex, he grabbed her wrist. "What are you planning?"

The man was tough but the hint of worry in his voice was unmistakable. "I've got to cut the pants off."

His iron grip eased and he released her. However, his body remained tense, as if ready to spring. Slowly she lowered the blade to cut off his pants. His flat belly flinched as the cold steel touched his skin. She sliced the fabric, moving down the pant leg all the way to the ankle. The pant leg fell open like a gutted fish. Grabbing the folds, she ripped the rest of the fabric up to his hip bone.

Blood oozed from a deep wound on the outer part

of his thigh. She prayed she'd not struck an artery. "This isn't going to be easy to fix."

"Do what you need to," he said, his voice a harsh whisper.

She removed a thick stick from her box and lifted it up to his lips. "So you don't bite your tongue off."

His eyes sharpened and for a moment she thought he'd refuse. Finally he opened his mouth. Even white teeth clamped down on the stick.

She studied the wound. The buckshot had torn away a portion of his thigh. She rolled him onto his side and inspected the back of his leg. There was no exit wound. The pellets had lodged deep and the bleeding was heavy.

He grunted as she rolled him back. "I've got to dig the pellets out, Mr. Baron. I'll do this as quickly as I can."

He nodded.

She prodded the wound with her fingertip. Every muscle in his body strained with pain.

Grimacing, she lifted the blade to the wound and started to dig. The marshal groaned. He squeezed his eyes shut and arched back against the pillow.

The tip of her blade grazed several pellets. The marshal swallowed and squeezed the handle of his pistol. Sweat beaded on her brow. *Please, let me get these out.*

Finally she wedged the blade tip under the bits of metal and, with a flick of her wrist, raised them up enough so that she could get the cluster out with her fingers.

By the time she'd removed the last, her hands and the sheets were soaked in blood. "That'll do it."

Sweat discolored Marshal Baron's shirt. His heartbeat thrummed rapidly at the base of his neck. His eyes remained shut and his brow knotted.

Ellie took the gun from his near lifeless hand. "I've got to wash the wound and stop the bleeding."

He didn't protest the taking of his gun this time. Like her, he seemed to understand that the cleaning would be worse.

She took the whiskey bottle and poured a liberal portion over the wound. The marshal hissed in a breath and groaned. Weakened by blood loss and pain, he passed out.

She pressed a white cloth against the wound, holding it in place for a half hour. Slowly the bleeding eased.

She rinsed the blood from her hands in the basin and then wiped them dry. Very carefully, she stitched and bandaged the wound.

When she was finished, the sun had dipped a bit lower in the sky. By her guess, it was past three o'clock.

Her gaze drifted back up to the hard planes of Nick Baron's face. Even in sleep he scowled. Few men could have endured the pain. Even Chin Lo would have been impressed.

She brushed back a lock of thick black hair from his forehead. A small scar marked his right brow and another trailed his jawline. Other scars were visible on his well-muscled arm and another on his shoulder blade.

The marshal wasn't a stranger to pain.

Sighing, she rose and stretched the tightness from her lower back. "You should have listened to me and left."

He shifted in his sleep, muttering something she didn't understand.

Ellie checked on the baby, who was still asleep. Three hours was a long nap for Rose and she'd soon wake up. While she still had the time, Ellie sat at the marshal's bedside. They were going to have a long night together. The next twelve hours would be critical. He could still hemorrhage or, worse, fever could poison his blood.

After a time, the baby woke and Ellie fed her. She cleaned Rose up and placed her back in her crib, then made herself a simple meal before she took up her post at the marshal's side again.

Later, she did her evening chores, feeding the animals and closing the place up for the night. Again, she fed Rose. Around midnight, she collapsed into a chair by the marshal's bed, her body so weary her bones ached.

Hours later a rooster crowed, waking Ellie. She jumped to her feet. Sunlight streamed into the cabin. She'd slept the night through in the chair. Immediately she checked the marshal, half expecting to find him dead. To her relief, he still breathed evenly. Her doctoring job seemed to have worked, for now.

Ellie stretched her arms, stood, and peeked in on the still-sleeping baby. Every muscle in her back ached. Coffee. She needed hot, strong coffee if she hoped to get through the day. She went to the kitchen, stoked the fire in the stove, set the coffee-pot on the burner and ground the beans. It would be an hour before the coffee was ready and the horses needed to be fed.

Her eyes itched as she went outside. The air was pleasantly warm. Normally she'd have savored a summer day like today.

As she crossed the yard toward the corral, chickens pecked the ground. An old cat rose from his bed of hay by the porch, yawned and followed her. A wild dog barked in the distance.

Her body protested as she loaded hay into the feed bins and hauled fresh water from the well near the barn. How had Annie been doing this alone for twenty years?

The whinny of a horse had her turning. Standing in front of the house was the marshal's mount. It pawed at the dirt and snorted.

She walked toward the black mare and whistled. The horse's nostrils flared.

"Of course," she muttered. "Why would the horse be less difficult than the man?"

The birds sang and a gentle breeze flapped the edges of her homespun skirt. She whistled again. "I won't hurt you!"

Again, the horse didn't move toward her. Sighing, she started toward the porch. "When you're ready, let me know. I'm too tired to fuss with you now."

As she climbed the first porch step, she heard the bridle jingle. She turned. The horse held its head high and proud, as if it were waiting for her. Its tail swished.

"Cocky thing, aren't you?" she said.

The horse snorted as if she were a queen.

Ellie lifted a brow. "Remember, I grew up around difficult women."

She moved slowly toward the horse. The mare's black eyes widened. "I can take that heavy saddle off and turn you loose into the corral. Sweet hay to eat."

The horse snorted again and took a step back.

Ellie hadn't ridden much in her life and if truth were told, she didn't like horses much. She'd heard they each had personalities, but she'd yet to figure one out.

"Your choice, gal. I'm not dealing with any more ornery creatures today." She stepped closer.

The horse didn't move this time. Gently, Ellie took hold of her reins and guided the mare toward the corral. It didn't take her long to unsaddle the horse. In the last two months, she'd saddled and un- saddled more horses than she had in the rest of her lifetime.

Fifteen minutes later the horse was watered and fed. She carried the marshal's saddlebag into the house and laid it on the table. She flipped open the thick buckle. "Let's just see what you're about, Mar- shal."

She dumped the bag's contents onto the table. She found two books, extra bullets, a knife sheathed in a fine leather case, a spare pair of handcuffs, an- other pair of pants and two extra shirts.

She picked up the knife and removed it from its soft sheath. The steel blade curved at the tip into a savage point and glistened in the sunlight. No doubt it could cut through most anything. Carefully she re- placed the blade.

Ellie's gaze dropped to the richly bound book. She

leafed through the pages. Her reading skills were limited, but she could see by the small letters that the book was the kind a very educated man read.

She glanced toward her room, where the marshal slept. The few lawmen she'd known hadn't had much formal education. "Mr. Baron, you are full of surprises."

Ellie wondered how long it would take her to finish a book like this. As slow as she read, it would probably take more spare time than she had in a year.

As Ellie leafed through the book, a tintype fell out. The edges were worn but the picture was clear. It was a wedding portrait of the marshal and a woman.

He was married. For some reason, the realization didn't sit well.

"What do you care?" she muttered. "The man's pure trouble."

Good sense didn't ease her curiosity. She studied the picture more closely. The marshal's face was downright boyish and there was a light in his eyes that testified to youthful energy. He wore a fine black suit, starched collar and silk tie.

She'd not have believed this was a picture of him if she'd not had time to examine it and see the same cleft chin and square jaw.

In the picture, the marshal stood with his hand

resting on the woman's shoulder. The woman wore a white dress trimmed in satin ribbons and on her head was a veil made of lace. A cameo threaded through a silk ribbon hung around her neck. She sat bolt-straight, her delicate hands folded in her lap. Her ice-blond hair was coiled on top of her head and tiny pearl-drop earrings dangled from her ears. Clear, pale eyes stared at the camera and her lips curled into a soft smile.

The girls at the Silver Slipper liked to dress up fancy but none had come close to looking like this woman. She possessed an air of quality and breeding that only came with real money.

Ellie looked at her own hands. Chapped by the wind and callused from work, they were not even remotely delicate. And her red hair, tied back at the nape of her neck, wasn't flat and smooth like the woman's. It curled into little ringlets when it rained. Her dress—a hand-me-down from the minister's wife in Butte—was two sizes too large and stained with grease.

Ellie flipped the picture over. "Crystal, 1872" was written in bold, black lettering.

Crystal. A pretty name.

She smoothed her fingertip over the image. There was more to the marshal than she'd first thought. He'd clearly lived a very different, refined kind of life.

Suddenly, Ellie felt very plain and very aware that she was the daughter of a whore. She'd never wear a fancy wedding dress or sit for a portrait. Silly to sit here and dream of the impossible.

She replaced the picture in the book and set about doing her chores.

DEMONS CHASED NICK into the fiery depths of hell. Or so he thought as he pushed the sheets and blankets away from him. Stifling heat seared his lungs and made it difficult to breathe. Sweat drenched his body.

As he battled to hang on to rational thought, Crystal stepped out from the darkness. Her flowing white hair draped her slender shoulders and her white transparent gown hugged her lush curves and teased her trim ankles. She was as stunning as he remembered and her smile as bright as a thousand stars.

Crystal. She was his wife and he loved her.

He held out his hand to her. Ah, if given a second chance he'd have spent more nights dancing with her, more afternoons making love to her and more mornings listening when she spoke. She leaned close to him, pressing her breasts to his chest. He could smell the lavender in her hair. "I love you," she whispered.

"I love you," he said. His body grew hard and he wanted to take her in his arms and make love to her.

But as he pulled Crystal close, time shifted and she vanished.

Out of the mists stepped his brother Gregory. They'd served together in the army, fought enemies together and drunk together. But Gregory was no friend. His older brother with the smiling green eyes had betrayed him with his wife.

Nick called out to Gregory. "Traitor. Animal. If I see you again, I will kill you."

Gregory laughed, his eyes glistening in the light. Nick watched his wife kiss Gregory as only lovers do.

Nick fisted his fingers. Outrage at the betrayal, still as fresh as an open wound, singed his veins.

Cool fingers brushed the hair from his forehead. "Shh. Shh."

Nick pried his eyes open and looked up through the haze. A woman with skin as pale as snow and hair as vibrant as the setting sun stared down at him. She smiled. He knew her, but from where he could not say. Her eyes were the color of green fields.

"What happened to me?" he said.

"You are safe. You must drink." She held a spoon up to his mouth and poured cool water into his mouth. The water trickled down the side of his face to the pillow.

"No!" He felt as if he were drowning.

"You must drink. It will break the fever." Again she held the spoon to his mouth. This time a bit of water seeped through his lips to his swollen tongue. It tasted refreshing. The next time she brought the spoon to his mouth, he opened his lips a fraction.

"That's good," she coaxed.

"Where am I?" he asked. He swallowed, his throat as dry as dust.

"You are safe, Marshal. Don't worry." She cradled his head in her hand and raised a cup to his mouth. The cool water soothed his parched throat and dry lips.

Why did she call him marshal?

The question was on the tip of his tongue, but he couldn't manage to speak the words.

His hand slid down his hip to where his gun normally hung. He realized the weapon was gone. He always had it with him, even when he slept. Without it he felt naked, vulnerable.

What the devil had happened?

Anger goaded him to sit up. The fire in his leg forced him back against the pillows. His eyelids felt very heavy.

Gregory, Crystal and finally the redheaded siren started to drift away. Sleep clouded his mind.

He didn't want the redhead to leave. He had to tell her something. But as hard as he tried to remain awake, the waves of sleep washed over him.

So many details escaped him, but one point was clear in his mind.

He and the siren were running out of time.

CHAPTER FOUR

By DAWN of the third day, the marshal's fever showed no signs of letting up. He continued to thrash and to call out to the woman named Crystal.

Red-orange light streamed through the window as Ellie moved across the cabin with a basin of fresh water. The baby still slept and she was careful not to make noise.

Water sloshed on Ellie's hands as she set the bowl beside the bed. She glanced down at the marshal. His olive skin remained sickly pale. She laid the back of her hand against his forehead. So hot.

She pulled clean cloths from her frayed apron pocket and sat on the edge of the bed. He murmured something she couldn't understand as she dipped a rag in the cool water and wrung it out. Gently she dabbed the cloth on his forehead.

She'd worked so hard to save him these last two and a half days. But fear of the hangman's noose no longer drove her. Pride had kept her going past exhaustion.

This man would not die. And she would win.

After rinsing the cloth in the water again, she pressed it to his cheek. Immediately his head turned toward her. His eyes remained closed and he mumbled more words that made no sense.

Ellie wiped his face, moving the rag over his strong jaw covered in a thick mat of dark stubble. She brushed his black hair off his forehead.

Even in sleep, his full lips curved down into a frown. He reminded her of the bare-knuckle boxers who fought in front of the saloon when the circus came to town.

He was so different from the boy she'd seen in the picture. What had happened to change him so?

Despite her better judgment, her curiosity about the man grew each day. She took the few clues she had to his past and wove story after story to explain how he'd ended up in Montana so far from his wife. He spoke of Crystal often in his sleep. A beautiful wife, a sound education and a marshal's badge. None of it made sense.

She continued to wipe his neck and chest. Keeping his body cool would be critical. If she could have, she would have dunked his entire body in cold water to break the fever.

She glanced at his torn pants. She'd left them on these last couple of days, but the time had come to strip him down. She chewed her lip as she stared at his belt buckle.

"Oh, for pity's sake, Ellie," she said. A girl born and raised in a brothel, she had seen her share of men in all states of undress. And she'd heard the girls talk about their customers, often laughing as they compared their attributes. But as much as Ellie had seen and heard, she had never *touched* a naked man.

She set down her cloth. "How bad can it be?"

Ellie pulled a sheet over his legs and covered his more private regions. She reached under the sheet for his belt buckle and unfastened it. The marshal's flat belly rose and fell with each breath. Coarse hair brushed her knuckles.

She moved to the foot of the bed and grabbed his pant legs. She started to pull. The pants didn't move. She tugged harder. Nothing.

Ellie blew a stray curl off her face. "I don't suppose you could lift your hips?"

Unconscious, he didn't respond.

Ellie moved to the middle of the bed, reached under the sheets and grabbed his waistband. His skin was warm beneath her fingers. Keeping her gaze averted, she tugged. The pants started to slide down his hips. So did the sheet. Then the pants caught on the bandage.

She dropped her gaze.

Her cheeks flamed.

This man was well constructed. The girls at the Silver Slipper would have done their best to attract his attention. They'd have called him a Handsome Devil.

She covered him with the sheet and gingerly worked his pants off. She tossed them on the floor.

Without warning, his arm captured her wrist and he pulled her against him. Her lips were but inches from his. Then he lifted his lips to hers.

He tasted salty and sweet and soft and hard all at the same time. Smoldering embers in her body ignited. Heat spread from the core of her body through her limbs. She relaxed into the kiss and savored the taste of his lips and the feel of his body.

"Crystal," he murmured, his eyes closed. His hand dropped away.

She pulled back, feeling a thousand times the fool.

Here she sat kissing a man who not only belonged to another woman, but who had brought nothing but trouble to her life. Lord, but she was a pitiful, weak-willed creature.

She rose from the edge of the bed, wanting nothing more than to put distance between them.

At least he'd been asleep when they'd kissed. He wouldn't remember a thing.

If only she could forget.

OVER THE NEXT FEW DAYS, Ellie fell into a routine. She cleaned the marshal's wound, drained it and watched for gangrene, which blessedly never showed.

Early in the morning of the sixth day, the marshal's fever had eased a little. It looked as if his body would fight off the infection. He would live.

This realization fostered a new set of worries. What if she couldn't convince him that she didn't have Frank's gold? Would he take her to jail? Could he take Rose away? He'd already proven himself hardheaded and single-minded.

Gathering the logs she'd just split, she walked up to the porch and inside the house. The door to his room remained ajar, as she'd left it. The sound of his deep, even breathing filled the house.

She set the logs in the box by the fireplace and then, wiping her hands on her apron, looked down into the cradle at Rose. Since the marshal had taken over her room, she'd moved the cradle out to the main room. At night, she slept on a pallet by the cradle so that she'd be close to the marshal.

The floorboards creaked behind her and she whirled around. The marshal stood in the center of the cabin, buck-naked. He leaned heavily against the wall, careful to keep the weight off his injured leg.

Her gaze darted from his wild eyes to his well-muscled chest. She didn't dare look any lower.

Her womb tightened and a hot restless feeling settled in the pit of her stomach. She remembered their kiss and heat rose in her cheeks.

"I want my gun!" the marshal shouted.

Shocked back to her senses, Ellie snapped her mouth shut. Color flooded her face.

"Gun!"

The marshal squinted at her. *"Pistol."*

Her mind cleared. "Oh."

In a low growl full of menace, he repeated himself. "My gun, Ellie."

She lifted her chin, but held her ground. "No guns at the coach stop. It's Miss Annie's policy."

The marshal took a step toward her. *"Gun!"*

Rose started to cry. Ellie scooped up the baby. She glared at the marshal, all traces of desire gone. "You can't have your gun," she said, as if speaking to a child. "When you're ready to leave, I'll give it to you."

"Damn you, woman, I'm in no mood to argue." He pressed his fingers to his temple as if talking hurt. "There are men who'll kill me if they catch me defenseless."

She lifted an eyebrow, unmoved. "Is that supposed to scare me?"

"They'd also kill you and that baby of yours just for fun."

A cold chill snaked down her spine. It had been

a fluke she'd hit him. If there were others, she might not be as lucky defending herself and Rose.

"You will be safer *with* me armed," he said, as if he'd read her thoughts.

She suspected he was right. With Rose cradled close to her, she went to a chest behind the dining table. "It's in there."

He limped to the chest and retrieved the gun. He snapped open the chamber and turned the cylinder. Satisfied his gun remained loaded, he snapped it closed.

"Anyone else come by the stop since I've been here?"

"No. Frank Palmer might not find me out here."

"He will." He closed his eyes for a moment.

She kept a respectful distance. Injured predators could still move quickly. "I told you I don't know anything about the gold."

He swayed. "He doesn't know that."

Her next retort died on her lips when she noticed the red stain on his bandage. "You're bleeding."

The marshal glanced down. Neither the blood nor his nudity seemed to bother him. "A little blood doesn't matter."

She laid the baby in her crib. "You don't have an ounce to spare. It's a wonder you didn't bleed to death."

"I'm fine."

Stubborn, stubborn man. She wrapped her arm around his waist. He felt as hot as a fritter.

He gave her a good bit of his weight. "If it weren't for Frank Palmer headed this way, I couldn't care less if you passed out. You're easier to deal with when you're out cold. But I need you healthy so that you can keep my baby and me alive."

He touched his bandage and grimaced. "Woman, anyone ever tell you you're a pain in the ass?"

She guided him back to his bed. "More times than I can count."

When he sat back down on the bed, he was pale and his white bandage—which she'd only just changed—was stained crimson.

"You've gone and torn one of my nice, neat stitches, mister," she murmured.

He ground his teeth as if he were in pain. Few men could have risen from the bed at this stage of the healing process, let alone walked. He lay back against the pillows and she lifted his feet onto the bed before covering him with a sheet.

Taking scissors from her basket, she knelt beside the bed and uncovered his wounded leg. "I went to a lot of trouble to save your life and I'd hate to see my efforts go to waste."

Her saucy tone had his eyes narrowing. "You're the one who shot me."

She shrugged. "I told you to stop."

Gingerly, she worked the tip of the scissors under the gauze. She could feel the marshal tense and suspected if she did anything threatening, he'd act.

"Would you relax? I feel as if I'm ministering to a wounded bear. If I were gonna kill you, I'd have done it long ago."

He released the breath he held. "I am relaxed."

"You're back is about as stiff as one of these floorboards."

He grunted.

Her cutting complete, she slowly peeled the fabric away. She leaned closer to get a better look at his leg.

"I think you've only ripped the top stitch. If I bandage the wound tightly enough, and you stay in bed, the bleeding should stop."

"I feel like I've been run over by a herd of buffalo."

"You're lucky to be alive." She took a jar from her basket and scooped out some ointment. She probed the wound with her finger. "By the looks of things, I'd say I did a good job patching you up."

"Am I supposed to thank you?"

Slowly she started to spread the ointment over the wound. "It wouldn't be out of line."

"You're joking," he grumbled.

"No."

She wound a smaller bandage around his leg. Her breasts grazed his knee as she reached around his leg to wrap the bandage. The touch sent a thousand prickles down her spine. It was one thing to nurse a man when he was out cold, but quite another when he was awake and staring at her.

She stepped back, her cheeks flushed. Lord, but she was acting like the silly girls she used to watch giggling by the schoolhouse.

The marshal saw the color in her cheeks. "You don't make sense."

"What do you mean?"

His gaze bore into her. "You shot me and then took better care of me than most doctors."

She felt color creeping up her cheeks. "I'm not a cold-blooded killer, Mr. Baron. If you'd told me you were a marshal, I wouldn't have shot you. And the idea of hanging for murder doesn't sit too well with me."

"There's more to it than that." He captured a stray curl of hers between his fingers.

Caught off guard, she didn't know how to react. He was out of line, still slightly feverish, and yet she wanted nothing more than to close her eyes and rub her cheek against his callused hand.

"You know, from the moment I first saw you, I've wondered what your hair would look like down."

The rawness in his voice stunned her. No man had ever made her feel more alive.

"If I were healthier, I'd want you in this bed with me." His voice was like raw silk.

The idea of lying beside him made her core tighten. She moistened her lips. A lady likely would be outraged and would tell him to mind his manners. But she didn't know the first thing about being a lady.

"Do you know what I'd do to you if you were beside me?"

Ellie couldn't speak as her cheeks flamed. The thought that this man wanted her scared and excited her.

He chuckled. "I've never seen a whore blush."

Whore. His bluntness shattered the moment.

Embarrassed and ashamed, she pulled away. She was acting like a whore. Anger nipped at her insides. What had she thought? That he'd wanted more than just sex. Her romantic notions were beyond foolish.

Men like the marshal took what they wanted and then moved on. She'd seen his kind a thousand times.

"What's wrong?" he said. "A tumble would do us both good."

She'd never felt cheap before, but she did now. "No thanks."

He looked genuinely confused by her shift in demeanor. "I'll pay, if that's what's bothering you."

"Keep up that kind of talk, mister, and I just might shoot you again."

NICK HAD NOT wanted to fall asleep, but he did shortly after Ellie had changed his bandage. He didn't wake until midday. Sweat covered his body, but his mind had cleared and his fever had broken.

His entire body hurt. He wanted nothing more than to lie in bed. He needed sleep. He needed to take it easy.

But as he lay staring at the door that separated his room from the rest of the cabin, he was very aware of the silence. He didn't hear Ellie or the baby.

He'd spoken to Ellie—said something that had made her mad—but for the life of him he couldn't remember what it was.

Alarm kicked his senses into high gear. Could Ellie have left with the baby?

He tried to reason the thought away. But an overwhelming sense of unease gripped him.

And then he remembered that when he'd been feverish, he'd offered to buy an hour of her time. She'd not been pleased. Damn. What the hell had gotten into him?

"Ellie!"

Nothing. He waited another beat and then shouted louder. "Ellie!"

Again nothing.

Where the devil had she gone? "Ellie!"

Rose started to cry as if she'd been startled awake. He hated waking the child, but the sound of her cries offered a measure of relief. If the baby was here, Ellie would be close and she would come running at the sound.

When he didn't hear her enter the cabin, he knew something was wrong.

He pushed himself up on his elbows. Pain shot up from his leg and for a moment it nearly took his breath away. Sweat beaded on his forehead. But as the seconds ticked by, the pain lessened and he shifted into a full sitting position.

Rose's cry grew louder.

He grabbed a blanket off the chair beside his bed and draped it around his shoulders. Gritting his teeth, he slid his leg over the side of the bed. Even in the August heat, the floor felt cool on his bare feet.

He sucked in a breath, stood and shuffled into the great room. There was no sign of Ellie, but he could see Rose in her cradle by the hearth. Her face was red and her tiny fingers were clenched into fists.

Nick hobbled across the floor. The distance to the cradle might as well have been twenty miles. His heart pumped in his chest and his muscles cramped from the exertion.

When he reached the cradle he sat on the rope chair beside it, more grateful than he could say to have the weight off his leg. He clutched the blanket around him with one hand and rocked the cradle with the other.

Rose cried louder. The baby had Jade's reputed temper.

"Shh," he said. "It's all right." He looked out the window, hoping to see some sign of Ellie. "I sure would like to know where the devil your mother is." He jiggled the crib harder.

Rose's sobs stopped. "Just looking for a little attention?" His voice sounded calmer than he felt. "I had a sister, Julia, like you. She was fine as long as someone was paying attention to her, but the minute you left her alone, she started to fuss." The baby's cries softened. She started to chew on her fist.

Nick thought about Julia. When he'd left Virginia ten years ago, she'd been nine years old. "She's got to be all grown up. She could be married with children by now." The thought that he'd missed so much of her life saddened him. Julia had been the only one in his family who hadn't wanted him to leave. He pinched the bridge of his nose, amazed how his life had gone so very differently than he'd ever imagined.

He stopped rocking the cradle and eased his hand back. Immediately, Rose started fussing. He jiggled the cradle again, but this time she didn't stop grizzling.

He steadied the crib, reached in and picked her up. She was lighter than a feather, yet he could feel the strength in her. He laid the baby on his shoulder and started to pat her on the back. "Shh," he whispered in her ear. "I can tell you, if your mama doesn't get here soon, we're going to have to go and look for her." If Frank was out there and he laid a hand on Ellie, he'd kill the bastard.

Footfalls sounded on the steps and Ellie appeared in the door. She wore a wide-brimmed straw hat, carried a basket filled with an odd collection of herbs and her shotgun. Her gaze locked on him and the child. "What are you doing?"

He continued to pat the baby on the back. "I could ask you the same. Where have you been?"

She set the basket and gun down and crossed the room. She took Rose from him. To his surprise, he missed the warmth of the child against his chest.

"Is something wrong with the baby? I'd put her

down for her morning nap and she never wakes for at least an hour."

"I might have woken her. When I didn't see you in the cabin, I called out to you." Ellie smelled of fresh air and sunshine.

"I went to the edge of the woods to collect some herbs and roots to make a paste for your leg."

"You shouldn't go so far. Frank could be anywhere."

She frowned. "I took my shotgun."

"Frank won't come at you head-on like I did. He'll come out of nowhere. He'll have that gun out of your hands before you even know what happened."

Her face paled a fraction. The baby, without a care in the world, had fallen asleep on her shoulder. "I hate this whole situation."

"I'm not so partial to it myself. But it's what we got to deal with." Sitting up this long had drained what little strength he had and, despite his efforts, his shoulders started to sag.

"We best get you back to bed," Ellie said, laying the baby down. She wrapped her arm around his shoulder and helped him stand. She nestled her body close to his so that she had a firm grip on him, though he doubted she could support his weight if he did fall. She was such a little bit.

He grunted, hating the weakness in his body.

Slowly they moved across the cabin. When she eased him onto the bed, he felt as if he'd run ten miles.

"Don't worry. You will be your old self soon enough."

He glanced up at her, surprised she had read his thoughts.

She caught his expression and smiled. "You're an open book."

He lay back on the pillow. "I am *not* an open book." Hell, how many times had he bluffed his way through a bad poker hand or around an outlaw when his gun was out of bullets?

She tucked the blanket under his chin. "You were worried about me, weren't you? I could see it on your face."

Had he been that transparent? Damn, he was losing his touch.

She laughed.

CHAPTER FIVE

WHEN NICK WOKE, the sun was low in the sky, bathing the cabin in orange and red light. He didn't know how long he'd been asleep, but his leg no longer burned with pain.

Sitting up slowly, he swung his legs over the side of the bed. For a second, he paused, until the swimming sensation eased and his body adjusted to sitting up. From the corner of his eye, he saw his gun on the bedside table.

The faint smell of stew filled the cabin.

He glanced down at his naked body. He'd have to find his clothes.

Dragging a blanket with him, he wrapped it around his waist and stood. Immediately his leg started to throb. The pain forced him to lean against the wall and ease the weight from his injured limb, but he was heartened to realize the ripping pain he'd endured days ago hadn't returned. Good. He was healing. Now if he could just find Ellie.

A large walking stick leaned against the cabin wall. A sign of Ellie. He sensed she wasn't far. Damn, did the woman ever stay in one place?

He limped outside. The cool, fresh air smelled sweet.

Ellie sat in a rocker, her back to the front door. Her hair hung loose, past her shoulders. As he stepped closer, he realized she had a nursing bottle in the baby's mouth.

The sight of Ellie holding the baby stirred images and emotions he'd thought long forgotten.

She glanced up. "It's good to see you moving about. How does your leg feel?"

"Better."

"Good."

He'd not realized until this moment how young she looked—perhaps not even twenty years old. "Where are my clothes?"

"I'll get them." She stood and he could see she was dressed in the same frayed dress she'd worn when he arrived. The garment hid the full curve of her breasts and her narrow waist. He'd seen women draped in silks, furs and jewels who had not looked half as stunning as Ellie did now. His body hardened and he was grateful for the blanket draped around his waist.

"No need, just point the way," he said, his voice gruff.

"Be easier if I showed you." Carrying the baby, she walked inside. "I did laundry yesterday."

Yesterday. "How long have I been sleeping?"

She nodded to the clothes in a neat stack at the edge of her bed. "This time? Only about six hours."

"And since I've been shot?"

"Six days."

"Six days!" He'd never lost time like this before and it was unsettling.

"Six days is nothing. Most men would have been out for weeks."

He wasn't appeased. Instead he thought of Frank. The bastard could be anywhere.

"I washed your clothes. They were a mess. Blood splattered up onto your shirt and it took a good bit of scrubbing to get it out. There was no saving your pants but I found a second pair in your saddlebag, which I cleaned."

The baby stirred in her arms and she pulled the bottle from her mouth, set it on the table and lifted Rose to her shoulder. She patted her on the back until she burped.

Nick's heart tightened. Clearly, Ellie loved the child, and Frank would use that love to get his gold. The outlaw would kill the child if need be. Nick knew he'd never let that happen.

"There's water in the basin in your room," Ellie said, moving toward the stove. "And I've stew on the stove. Once you've dressed, I'll make a plate for you. And be mindful of that wound or you'll rip every stitch."

Clearing his throat, he retreated to his room. The sooner he dressed and ate, the better help he'd be to Ellie. They'd all been damn lucky so far that Frank hadn't shown up.

But he knew their luck would run out sooner rather than later.

As THE MARSHAL dressed, Ellie's nerves danced on the edge as she ladled the stew onto a tin plate. Unconscious, his presence filled the cabin. Awake, it dominated.

The worries that had festered since his arrival grew threefold. She didn't want any part of a hunt for Frank. She wanted to live a normal life with Rose.

She'd stayed these last six days because Nick had needed her. But soon he'd be able to care for himself. And her chances of escaping him narrowed each day. If she and Rose were going to run, it would have to be very soon.

Ellie sighed as she laid the baby in her cradle. She didn't want to run. She liked working at the coach stop with Annie. This house had been more of a home in two short months than the Silver Slipper had been in twenty years.

But she couldn't afford sentimentality now. If the marshal could find her, so would Frank.

She had to run. But to where?

Her limited options frustrated her. She couldn't return to Butte and the town of Thunder Canyon was too close. If only she did have Jade's gold. She and Rose would go far away to a big city like Denver or Chicago and buy a place just big enough for the two of them.

But she didn't have Jade's gold. She'd have to find work.

With a plate of hot stew in hand, Ellie turned toward the table. She started, nearly dropping her plate, when she saw the marshal standing there. He wore black from head to toe and he'd combed back his hair and washed his face. He looked good.

Hot stew sloshed onto her skin and burned her hand. Quickly she set the plate on the table and reached for a rag.

"You all right?" he said.

"My word, you move as quiet as a cat."

"Old habit." He stared down at her. "Forgive me."

The regret in his eyes looked genuine and her anger softened. She suspected this man rarely apologized for his actions.

"Have a seat," she said, nodding to a chair.

Standing close to him, she felt the energy radiating from him. Tarnation, but breathing seemed harder when he stood close.

"Thank you," Nick said.

She was hungry but would wait until he'd finished. Miss Adeline had trained her to feed the customers first and then herself.

The marshal stood by his chair. "I won't eat until you sit."

Ellie glanced at him. She suspected his leg pained him. "What?"

"I do not eat while a lady stands."

Ellie's gaze followed his outstretched hand to the empty chair. The idea of sitting across from him made her skin prickle. "I've got plenty of chores to do. You go on and eat. I'll get something later."

"Make yourself a plate. Sit," he said. He stood military-straight.

Her nerves jumped. "It's a rule I have. I don't eat with the customers."

He shrugged. "Then make a new rule."

The determined set to his jaw suggested he was just stubborn enough to stand there all day. And frankly, she was hungry. Her stomach rumbled. Giving up, she fixed a plate and sat across from him. Only when she sat did he sit.

He took a bite of stew. "This is good," he said. He took another bite and another. He was half starved. "Thanks."

"No, this is very good." He took another bite.

"Eat up."

For several minutes they ate in silence. Normally she worked while she ate.

When her stomach was filled, her curiosity came alive. It would have been wise to leave Nick and let him eat his food—the less she knew about him, the better. But the questions got the better of her. "You're not from this area, are you?"

His tore a piece of bread. "No."

She set down her spoon. "Where are you from?"

"I doubt you know the place."

"Likely not. Butte is about all that I do know."

"I come from a small town in Virginia. It's called Ashland," he said after a moment's silence. "It's very far away."

"I won't pretend to know where it is. What brought you here?"

He lifted a brow. "A change of pace."

"It's been my experience men don't just move to Montana for a change. They're either looking to get rich quick or they're running from their past."

He didn't answer.

She thought about the books she'd found in his

saddlebags. "Most lawmen don't read the kind of books you got in your saddlebag."

"I suppose."

For a moment silence settled between them. The girls at the Silver Slipper said most men who came into the brothel liked to talk as much as they liked to diddle. Getting words out of Nick Baron was like pulling teeth.

The baby, who'd been napping in her cradle, woke. "Always at meals," Ellie muttered, rising.

Nick set his fork down and watched her pat Rose on the back. The child's fussing slowed, but Ellie could feel Nick's gaze on her.

"You are good with that baby," he said finally.

"I'm learning every day."

"What's her name?"

"Rose."

"Who named her?"

Ellie rocked the cradle. "Jade picked it."

"The stolen gold could buy a lot of nice things for the baby."

His comment caught her off guard. He was right. She had good reason to hide the gold from him, she silently acknowledged as she sat down. "It sure could. Problem is, I don't have it."

"If I were a woman alone, I'd keep the gold."

"I just might, too, *if I knew where it was.*"

"I can't believe Jade would go to her grave and not tell you about it."

"Gold was about the last thing on both our minds at the time."

"Jade was always thinking, from what I've heard. You can bet she hadn't forgotten about it."

The whinny of horses and the sound of hooves silenced Ellie's retort.

Nick tensed. "Are you expecting visitors?"

"It's a coach stop. We get visitors all the time."

"Visitors mean trouble."

"And revenue." A visitor could also help her escape Nick.

Ellie jumped to her feet and, before he could react, hurried outside without checking to see who had arrived.

NICK CURSED. The woman had sawdust for brains. She hadn't even bothered to look out the window to see who had ridden up. Hell, it could very well be Frank.

He winced as he rose. Resting his hand on his six-shooter, he limped toward the door.

But he didn't rush outside as Ellie did. He hid in the shadows. If this were one of Frank's traps, he'd not be able to save Ellie in a face-to-face confrontation with Frank. Injured, he needed surprise.

He pushed back the curtain. Two riders dismounted and sauntered to the base of the porch step. One was tall, lean, with a scraggly beard and beady eyes. The other had a thick waist and thin, black hair that hung past his shoulders.

Ellie moved toward the men, confident and unafraid. Fool. No woman in her right mind went to a stranger like that. Then it struck Nick that Ellie greeted strange men as a matter of course. At the Silver Slipper she'd most likely entertained her share. To his surprise, a bolt of jealousy burned his veins.

"Welcome," Ellie said. "You men passing through?"

The shorter of the two men hooked his thumbs into his thick gun belt. "You could say that. We passed through a couple of months ago. I'm Hugh and this is my friend Fat Pete."

Ellie smiled. "I remember. You paid Annie in gold dust."

"That's right," Hugh said.

"I'm glad you came back through. I've got stew on if you're hungry."

Hugh smiled, revealing broken yellowed teeth. "I was telling my friend Fat Pete, here, that I know you from some place else—that whorehouse in Butte, maybe."

Ellie folded her arms over her chest as her shoulders stiffened. "I don't think so. My late husband and I were from Denver."

Nick noted how easily she lied.

Hugh spit on the ground. "I don't know. It was about six months ago. We were at the Silver Slipper whorehouse. You served us supper."

Ellie tucked a coppery curl behind her ear, as if she were doing her best to look relaxed and uninterested. "I'm afraid you've made a mistake."

Fat Pete leaned closer. His eyes held a hunger Nick did not like. "Hugh never forgets a face, especially one that's as pretty as yours."

"You're wrong," Ellie said clearly. "I've never been to Butte."

Nick's hand slid to his gun.

Hugh moved a step closer. "We think you are lying."

Ellie's back stiffened. "I'm going to ask you two men to leave now."

"Once we've finished our business," Fat Pete said.

Nick could tolerate no more. Gun drawn, he stepped out of the shadows and onto the porch. Pain burned through his leg as he forced it to bear his weight. "She's already got a customer," he said quietly.

Ellie backed away from the edge of the porch toward Nick. This close, he could see she trembled.

Hugh took a step back. "I knew she was from Butte. I told you, Pete, I never forget a face."

Fat Pete laughed. "We'd be willing to wait. I never did mind sharing."

Nick bared his teeth in a dangerous smile. "I don't share."

Hugh's eyes narrowed. "Now that don't seem right. A good whore can do ten men in a night."

Nick cocked his gun. "Leave."

Hugh scowled as his hand slid to his gun. "The way I see it, there are two of us and one of you."

Nick fired his gun so quickly Ellie wasn't sure what had happened until she saw the plume of dirt at Hugh's feet and heard him yelp. "Try me."

"Damn, mister," Hugh said. "We don't want trouble, but if it's trouble you want—"

"I want your guns," Nick said.

"I ain't giving up my guns!" Hugh said.

Nick shrugged. "Your guns or your kneecaps. The choice is yours."

Fat Pete didn't have to be told twice. He dropped his gun belt. "He'll do it, Hugh. That's Nick Baron, the bounty hunter. The Tracker. I heard he skinned a man and left him for the coyotes just because the man spit on his boot."

Hugh hesitated. "A big reputation don't mean nothing to me."

Nick fired his gun. The bullet knocked Hugh's hat off his head. "The next one will be between the eyes."

Hugh shouted an oath as he reached for his belt buckle. His guns dropped to the ground.

"Ellie, get the guns," Nick ordered.

She didn't argue and collected the guns. She moved to stand some distance behind him.

He pointed his six-shooter at Fat Pete and Hugh as if he'd not decided whether he was going to kill them.

Hugh held up his hands. "We don't want any trouble."

"Then remove the rifles from your saddle scabbards and give them to me," Nick ordered.

"That'll leave us defenseless!" Hugh looked worried.

Nick fired his pistol again, nicking Hugh's ear. "Die now or later. It makes no difference to me. But I will have your guns."

Their eyes wide with fear, they scrambled to their horses and pulled the rifles from their holsters. Fat Pete set his on the ground immediately, but Hugh whirled around, raising his rifle.

Nick fired, hitting Hugh in the hand. The miner's rifle dropped to the dirt and he clutched his bleeding hand.

Ellie winced. She moved a step further away from Nick.

Hugh quickly laid his rifle in the dirt next to Fat Pete's. He clutched his wounded hand to his chest. "There, you got it. Now don't shoot no more!"

"Get on your horses and ride," Nick ordered. "If I see either of you again, I won't be so generous. I will kill you."

Neither argued. Fat Pete helped Hugh up on his horse and then mounted his. They rode off without a backward glance.

Nick kept his gaze on the riders, but he was aware that Ellie stared with horror. He'd cultivated and encouraged the legends about himself because he'd wanted people to be afraid of him. Fear made his job easier.

But seeing Ellie's naked apprehension troubled him deeply.

"Is what they said true?" she asked.

"Enough of it."

"You aren't a marshal."

"No."

A wrinkle furrowed her brow. "How do I know you're not working with Frank?"

"You don't."

CHAPTER SIX

LATER THAT EVENING as Ellie folded Rose's freshly laundered clothes, she mentally cataloged what she needed to take when she and Rose left.

There wasn't much, of course. A bottle, a few cans of milk, three baby gowns and the twenty dollars she'd earned these last few months. She owned the dress she wore and a store-bought one Annie had given her. She'd never worn the blue calico because it had just seemed too fancy for her, but she'd cherished the gift nonetheless.

In truth, there wasn't much she and Rose truly needed. As long as they had each other, they'd manage.

Nick's voice interrupted her thoughts. "I would never hurt you."

Ellie started and looked up. He stood by the stove, a cup of coffee in his hand. He stared at her. Self-consciously she wondered what had caught his attention and then she realized she'd been sorting the laundry—a pile to keep and a pile to leave behind.

"I don't know what you're talking about." She looked away but could still feel his gaze on her. Color flooded her cheeks as she put the piles into one stack and carried them to the chest by her bed. Absently she smoothed the wrinkles from the clothes Rose would never wear again.

Nick set his cup down. Lantern light flickered on the hard planes of his face. "I am the best hunter there is, Ellie."

"Why should I care about that?"

"Because you are planning to leave." His voice was smooth, unemotional and lethal.

Guilt and fear gnawed at her as she moved to the oven to pull out a loaf of freshly baked bread. She didn't mean to leave Annie, but Fat Pete had called him "The Tracker" and Rose had to come first.

In such a rush to pretend nothing was wrong, she didn't double fold her hot mitt. The scorching pan burned through to her fingers. She hissed and dropped the pan on the cook top.

Nick dampened a cloth with cool water and limped toward her.

She blew on her fingertips. "That's ridiculous. How far would I get with a baby?"

He wrapped the wet cloth around her fingers. "You made it here all the way from Butte. I didn't find you sooner because I underestimated you. I won't misjudge your determination again."

The pain in her fingertips coupled with frustration and fear brought sudden hot tears to her eyes. "I've told you, I don't have the gold. Good Lord, if I did have that kind of money, do you think that I'd be in a coach station working twelve hours a day?"

He turned her hand over. Her fingertips were red. Gently he held her hand above the washbasin and poured water from a pitcher over it. The throbbing in her fingers eased. She tried to pull her hand away but he held tight. "You are smart. I won't deny that."

"What does that mean?" she asked.

"It means you are patient. Perhaps you are waiting for Frank and people like me to forget about the money."

She rolled her eyes. "It's been my experience that people don't *forget* about twenty thousand dollars. I saw a man shot in cold blood once for fifty cents. You can bet if I had the money I'd have bought a ticket to someplace very, very far from Montana."

He absorbed what she said. "You have always lived in Montana. It makes sense you wouldn't stray too far from it."

His hand was warm, callused. "The only thing Montana has given me is long days filled with hard work."

"Better to stay with the devil you know than the devil you don't know," he said softly. "It is hard to leave one's home."

She pulled her hand away, not liking the way her heart hammered in her chest when he touched her. "If I had twenty thousand dollars, I'd find it in me to leave."

He stared at her as if he were trying to read her thoughts. "Yes, I believe that you would."

The baby fussed and Ellie moved away from him, grateful for the reprieve. She picked the child up, savoring the soft scent of her skin. Rose calmed her nerves. Ellie warmed a bottle she'd already made up and teased the baby's lips open with the nipple. The gentle scent of milk wafted around her.

Nick folded his arms over his chest. His face held as much expression as a wall of granite. "How old are you, Ellie?"

"Nineteen, I think, this past spring."

He frowned. "You're not sure?"

"Adeline didn't bother with records when one of her girls gave birth."

"Your mother worked at the Silver Slipper, as well?" He sounded surprised.

"Ma arrived at the Silver Slipper two years before I was born, but she'd worked a dozen different saloons in Montana since she was twelve."

"How old were you when she died?"

"Six."

"And Miss Adeline kept you?"

"I didn't have any family and Miss Adeline thought I'd be of help in the kitchens."

"Why didn't you leave?"

She sighed. "I thought about it enough, but I didn't know where I'd go. At the Silver Slipper, I knew I'd at least be able to get a good meal and have a bed to sleep in each night." She pulled the bottle from Rose's mouth and checked to see how much she'd eaten. "And there was an old man I worked with in the kitchen, Chin Lo. We got on well and in his way he looked after me. As I got older, I talked to him about the both of us leaving, but he said he was too old to start over. So I stayed with him. He died about five months ago."

"What do you mean, he looked after you?"

"If a customer got out of hand with me, Chin Lo would slip him something to make him sick or sleep."

"Did you love him?"

"I don't know. I suppose."

Nick was silent for a moment. "When did you move to the upstairs work?"

Ellie laid Rose on her shoulder and patted her back. Everyone assumed Ellie was a whore. There'd been a time when she'd watch the proper ladies in town and try to copy their speech and the way they walked. But no matter how much she'd tried to be like a lady, no one thought any better of her. "*When* doesn't matter, does it?"

"I suppose not."

She could have told him that she'd never worked the upstairs rooms. Lord knew the money was better. But his assumption made her mad. She didn't feel as though she had to justify anything to Nick.

Ellie had decided when she was a young girl to guard that part of her that was only hers to give. Women had so little and it pained her to see them sell their souls for a couple of bits.

Nick sat in the chair by the stove, easing the pressure on his leg. He didn't say anything to her for the next half hour as she finished the baby's feeding. She wrapped up the last of her evening chores and locked the front door as she did every night. Leaving didn't mean she'd shirk today's chores. She'd give Annie her due until the moment she left.

She laid Rose in the cradle in the main room. Nick rose and walked to his room. As she stood, she didn't notice Nick approach with the handcuffs until it was too late. He clicked a cuff closed over her wrist.

Before she could speak, the second bracelet clinked closed—around Nick's wrist.

She jerked at the handcuff. "What have you done?"

There was triumph in his eyes but no satisfaction. "I won't get much sleep if I'm worried about you running. Now I don't have to worry."

She twisted the cuff. "I never said I was going to run."

"You didn't have to." His voice was whisper soft. "I just knew."

"You can't do this to me."

He shrugged. "I believe that I have."

Panic welled inside her at the thought of lying beside him in bed all night. "No!"

Her outburst startled the baby and Rose began to cry. Automatically, Ellie reached for her, but she found her right wrist immobile.

"I can't care for my daughter if I'm shackled to you!"

His gaze pinned her. "We will have to work together, I suppose."

The baby continued to wail.

"But what about my chores during the day? And my visits to the necessary?"

"We will be shackled only for the nights. In the day, I can watch you."

"No, no, no."

"The baby needs you," he said.

His complete control only stoked her temper. She pulled her fist back, ready to hit him square in the jaw.

Nick's reflexes were too fast for her. He caught her hand easily. "Do not try that again, Ellie."

The glint of steel in his eyes sent a chill down her spine. "I should have let you die."

Sadness and regret flickered in his eyes. "Pick up the baby. She needs her mother."

Swallowing, Ellie reached for her child. Nick moved with her, giving the chain the slack she needed. His hard shoulder brushed hers and she could feel his warm breath on her neck.

As she rubbed the baby's back, she prayed for the courage to get her child out of this mess safe and sound. Finally, Rose's eyes drifted shut and she fell back to sleep.

"She will sleep the night through, I think," Nick said. "That is good. We will need the rest."

Ellie faced Nick. "It's not practical for us to spend all night sitting up."

"We won't. We will lie in the bed together."

"But the bed isn't big enough for the two of us. I could accidentally kick you in my sleep and reopen your wound."

"I run a greater risk of injury chasing you through the night on horseback than sleeping with you."

Her cheeks flushed with anger. "Don't bet on it."

NICK DECIDED Ellie had more spirit in her than many of the soldiers he'd served with in the army and the outlaws he'd tracked. He understood her desperation and he'd liked to have accommodated her. But he could not afford to lose her now.

She probably didn't know where the money was. A practical woman, she would have used the money to get as far away from Montana as she could if she'd had the means.

It pleased him that she didn't have anything to do with the money. He wanted to believe she was an innocent in all this—that she'd never lied to him. She had pride and honor and he admired that.

But Frank Palmer didn't know that. He'd never believe that the gold's location had most likely died with Jade. Frank would believe that Ellie knew where it was. And soon he would come.

"I am tired," he said truthfully.

She glanced from his face to the bedroom door. "I'm not sleeping with you."

He lifted his wrist shackled to her. "You don't have much of a choice, do you?"

"I'm not going."

He reached for the baby. "She'll want to sleep with her ma."

Ellie brushed his hands aside and picked the baby up.

He picked up the cradle with his free arm, held out his arm and nodded toward the door. When she didn't budge, he took her arm in his and half dragged, half pushed her to the bedroom.

She stumbled over the threshold. He set the cradle down and she laid the baby in it. She faced him as if ready to fight, but he saw the panic in her eyes. "What if I need to go to the outhouse?"

"I'll go with you."

She looked mortified. "You wouldn't dare."

"Try me."

"This is awful!"

They could argue all night. Nick sat on the bed, forcing Ellie to sit. She tried to remain on the edge, her feet planted on the ground, but as he scooted toward the center, she had no choice but to follow.

The small mattress, stuffed with hay, was lumpy. Its size forced them to lie on their sides—she facing the outside, he spooned behind her, his manacled arm resting on her rounded hip. His weight mashed the bedding down and she slid back into him.

Her tight bottom pressed against him, reminding him that he'd been on the trail far too long. Her hair was the color of fire, yet as soft as butter. It brushed his cheek. He imagined it caught the sunlight and curled when it was freshly washed.

Nick sighed. He was taking himself down a dangerous path. Ellie was a job and nothing more. A tumble between the sheets would be pleasant—real pleasant—but the complications later wouldn't be.

Her breathing was quick and her body tight with tension. "I warn you, Mr. Nick Baron, if you try anything, I will bite and kick you."

He had no doubt she could be quite a hellcat. "I'm too tired and too sore to try much of anything, Ellie. Get some sleep."

She drummed her fingers on the mattress. "You've lied to me before."

His lips were close to her ear. "As I remember, you'd just shot me and I was bleeding to death."

"So we are back to that again."

He sighed. "Go to sleep."

"I can't sleep."

She tried to wiggle away but only managed to bump her bottom against his manhood. Sleep wouldn't find him anytime soon, either. "Try."

They lay in the dark for a good while before Ellie's breathing slowed. Despite her best efforts, her body was beyond exhaustion. She drifted off to sleep.

But sleep didn't come easily for him. Nick propped his head on his hand and then pushed a stray curl off her face. Pale moonlight streamed through the window above their heads, highlighting her red curls.

So young.

Nick guessed Ellie hadn't worked Miss Adeline's upstairs rooms long. Her eyes didn't possess the hardened glint of the experienced whores who'd been sitting in the parlor when he'd arrived at the Silver Slipper looking for Frank.

Many of the women at the brothel had been attractive. Adeline had a reputation for hiring the prettiest girls. But he'd not been drawn to the women in the seductive silk dresses. It was the fluff of calico that had bumped into him by the back door that had stirred his imagination these last months on the trail.

He couldn't shake Ellie from his thoughts.

And he couldn't say why.

Some might have called her plain, with her wild red hair and the ringlets that framed her face. Her eyes seemed to swallow her face. Her lips, so full and red, added a seductive quality that he found very intriguing. He'd wanted to know what those lips tasted like. He still did.

Her delicate skin had yet to be marked by the sun, years of drinking or too much tobacco. But those days would come. In her profession, thirty was old.

She flinched each time he touched her. No doubt, her experiences at the Silver Slipper hadn't been pleasant. He thought of other men kissing those lips and felt a flash of temper.

Nick captured a strand of her hair between his fingers. Silk. She tried to keep the curls bound at the back of her neck, but they had a life of their own. They wouldn't be subdued.

Releasing the curl, Nick groaned and lay back on the pillow. Why in God's name did he keep touching this woman's hair?

What he needed were a couple of hours in the sack with a woman—any woman—and then this preoccupation with Ellie would be gone. However, the idea of bedding a woman other than Ellie suddenly had no appeal.

He propped his head on his hand. His gaze dropped to her breasts. As she lay in bed, the loose fabric of her bodice had twisted, tightening over the delicate mounds that rose and fell in a way that had him hardening.

He realized then that she hid behind the yards of calico, the aprons and the severe hairstyles. She didn't want to be feminine. She didn't want to be noticed. That also explained why she always kept moving. Except to feed the baby, she rarely sat in one place for more than a few minutes.

Life in the brothel had done that to her. It had robbed her of her femininity. It had instilled such fear that she never allowed herself to rest.

"And why the devil do you care?" he muttered, rolling on his back.

He was losing his focus and drive, both of which had served him so well. They'd taken him through the ranks of the army. They'd gotten him past his wife's death and then the discovery of her betrayal. They had given him the strength to bury a dear friend and finish this final hunt.

Reaching inside his pocket, he pulled out a small key and unlocked his cuff. Carefully he scooted away from Ellie and rose from the bed.

Lighting a lantern, he picked up his book and, without thinking, walked to the cradle. He glanced down at the sleeping child.

Rose. A flower born among thorns. Just like Ellie.

The child deserved better.

Ellie deserved better.

He eased his still sore body into a chair and opened his book.

Focus and drive.

As long as he kept his mind on his goal, and off Ellie and Rose, he'd be just fine.

CHAPTER SEVEN

ELLIE WOKE TO LIGHT streaming into her room. Never could she remember feeling so very warm and comfortable. Her body felt like it was floating. She stretched her arms over her head.

She smelled fresh coffee and bacon. She must still be sleeping, because never in her life had she woken up to the smells of breakfast. She had always been the one who stoked the fires and warmed the cold kitchen.

Purposeful footsteps sounded in the cabin, shattering her bliss. She wasn't alone. She bolted upright.

Pushing a lock of hair off her face, she struggled to gather her thoughts. For several tense seconds she wasn't sure where she was. Slowly her mind cleared. Annie's cabin. *Rose.* Her gaze darted to the side of the bed where the baby slept in the cradle. Her fear eased a fraction.

Nick. They'd spent the night in the same bed handcuffed together! She glanced down at her wrist, expecting to see handcuffs. They were gone.

Rubbing her naked wrist, she tried to clear her fogged mind. When had she fallen asleep? She'd done her best to stay awake, but the warmth of his body had lulled her into a deep sleep. Normally she never slept more than three hours at a stretch, but last night she'd slept harder than she ever remembered. And by the looks of the sun, it was well past eight o'clock.

She stood. Where was Nick? He had been the person she'd heard moving around, hadn't he?

Still dressed in the oversize homespun dress she wore all the time, she walked to the front door and spotted Nick on the porch, staring out at the horizon. He held a cup of coffee.

A flash of unreasonable relief sparked in her as she stared at his broad shoulders. He hadn't left. The fact that she cared one way or the other about him irritated her. What the devil was wrong with her? Depending on any man was plain foolish.

Her movement had him turning. "Good morning," he said.

"I thought you'd left."

He grinned. "I'm a bad penny, Ellie." The smile softened his hard features and made him look devilishly handsome. "I always turn up where I'm least wanted."

"So I've noticed." His coloring was better and he looked too healthy to be a man shot only a week ago.

"Buck up, Ellie. The lure of that gold will have Frank here sooner rather than later and I'll be gone before you know it."

Relief mingled with unexpected sadness. She'd never felt more confused about anyone in her life.

The baby wailed, letting Ellie know she was awake. She moved back inside to her room. Rose kicked and squirmed contentedly until she caught sight of Ellie and then she started to cry. "I bet you're a hungry one."

The baby howled louder.

"Don't believe her," Nick said. He'd stepped into the cabin. "I fed her only an hour ago."

Ellie picked up Rose and didn't try to hide her shock. "You fed her?"

"Don't look so surprised."

"I just can't picture it, that's all."

"I wasn't always a bounty hunter. I had another life once."

She thought of the wedding picture in his saddlebag. The picture had been taken long ago, but that didn't mean he didn't have a wife waiting for him. Perhaps he had a few babies back home. Odd, but she'd never thought of him as *married*. So foolish.

He answered her unspoken question. "I was the oldest of three. My younger sister was fourteen years younger than me. I cared for her from time to time."

But what about Crystal? Not meeting his gaze, Ellie retrieved a fresh diaper, laid the baby on the bed and stripped her wet gown off. The baby flailed her arms and kicked.

Nick moved closer, seemingly interested in the baby. Ellie found the simple task infinitely more difficult. Her fingers fumbled with the small buttons and diaper pins. "I can't picture you with family."

"You've got a very narrow view of me."

"Maybe because you don't look like you could have ever been a child. I wouldn't have been surprised if you said Lucifer had molded you out of clay and put you on the earth to create trouble."

He laughed. "You mean for you."

"You're the one who stepped into my life and turned it upside down. I was doing fine until you showed up."

"Fine?" He shook his head. "You're holed up in a coach stop struggling to make ends meet. I'll bet every night you jump when you hear a sound outside or see a shadow move, waiting for Frank or Adeline to show up."

She lifted her chin, unwilling to admit he'd hit the nail on the head.

"Neither has found me yet."

"But you worry nonetheless."

She did. She worried about it each day.

"And what would you have done if Frank had showed up on your doorstep, demanding that gold map? Or if Adeline wanted to take you back to the Silver Slipper?"

"I'd have figured out something."

"Maybe, maybe not."

Quickly, Ellie finished changing the baby and lifted her on her shoulder. "I've to go to the barn and milk the cow. The old girl has got to be bursting."

Nick nodded. "I'll go with you."

"I doubt I could run far with a baby and empty pockets."

He lifted a brow, as if shocked by her retort. "I thought that I could help."

Her gaze traveled up and down his body, hardened by years in the saddle. "You, milk a cow?"

His gray eyes held hers. "I can hold the baby while you do. And I'd like to check on my horse."

The idea of giving him Rose didn't sit well. He'd fed her once and that was enough contact, as far as she was concerned. The less contact between them, the better. "Rose and I have a little routine when we milk the cow." With the baby propped on her shoulder, she started out the door.

Her skirts swirled around her feet and her uncombed hair teased the sides of her face. She wished she'd had time to brush her hair and rub tooth powder on her teeth, feeling more conscious of her appearance than usual. But she was already hours behind on her chores.

The wind had picked up.

"We're in for weather," Nick said. Despite his bad leg, he matched her pace easily.

The pale blue sky showed no signs of storms. "How can you tell?"

"Can feel it in my bones."

Some men had a knack for calling the weather and she didn't doubt Nick was one of them. "Annie said the valley had seen more than its share of storms this summer."

"Today's is going to be a big one."

"I'd best hurry, then. The cow is skittish and it doesn't take much to dry her milk up." Ellie moved into the barn, slowing her pace as her gaze adjusted to the dimmer light. Hay lay in a large pile by the front door. The low-ceilinged room had eight stalls, four on each side of the barn. The room smelled musty, earthy. Mice scrambled overhead in the loft. "Your horse is in the last stall. She's a temperamental one."

Nick strode to the stall. The horse came to him immediately, nudging his hand with her nose. "Aurora and I have ridden thousands of miles together. She's never let me down."

Ellie felt a stab of jealousy. "I've never been able to say the same about a horse or person."

Sadness sharpened his gaze. "You're cynical for one so young."

Balancing Rose on her shoulder, Ellie picked up her bucket and went into the first stall, where the cow stood. "No, just practical."

She set her bucket down and pulled down the blanket draped over the side of the stall. She rigged a sling between the sides of the stall and laid Rose in the center.

"I offered to hold the baby," he said, striding toward the stall.

"No need. Rose is happy to watch me milk."

He leaned against the entrance to the stall and tickled the baby's toes. She kicked and smiled.

His hair was brushed back off his face and she realized that he'd shaved. Her skin tingled as her gaze skimmed his full lips.

"You're an independent one, aren't you?"

She sighed. She didn't feel independent most times. She felt frightened and alone. "It's the only way to be."

"It's been my experience that women don't want independence, but marriage," he said.

She glanced up at him. She thought of the lovely Crystal. "I've seen too many women throw all their hopes in with a man and then see them crushed. Men just are not suited for marriage."

"Not all men leave their women," he said. His voice now held an edge.

"Then why aren't you with your wife?" she challenged. There, she'd asked the question that had plagued her since the moment she'd found the photo. But the instant she asked it, she felt foolish.

His eyes narrowed.

"I searched your saddlebag that first night. I was curious. I saw the picture."

For a moment she didn't think he was going to answer her. "She died ten years ago."

"Oh." Embarrassed, she started to milk the cow, but Crystal's story continued to swirl in her mind. "What happened?"

Silent, he stared down at Rose. "She died giving birth."

Her mind immediately returned to the night Jade had given birth to Rose. She'd not known Jade well, but the sadness had been so great. At least Rose had survived. "What of the child?"

"Died with his mother." His flat tone hinted of deeper emotions.

"I'm sorry." She did her best to lose herself in the rhythm of the milking. But Nick's presence invaded her senses. His scent, his presence, even the rhythm of his breathing, filled up her brain so that she couldn't think of anything else but him.

Rose started to yell, clamoring for attention.

Nick picked the baby up.

A surge of panic exploded in Ellie as he took Rose. Her body tensed, ready to fight.

"Relax," he said. "I won't drop her."

This time she didn't argue. He'd lost a wife and son. If holding Rose gave him a bit of comfort, then so be it.

"She doesn't weigh more than a boot." He tucked the baby into the crook of his arm.

"She's been a small one since day one." Ellie finished the milking and stood with the full pail. The milk sloshed over her hands.

"I'll carry the pail," he offered, grabbing the handle.

"No, you could rip a stitch. Just carry Rose. I'll manage the milk."

He held on to the bucket. "Lead the way. I think that bacon should be ready soon, and I'm hungry."

She walked beside him, careful not to move far away in case he stumbled or lost his hold on Rose.

He followed her up the front steps and into the house. He set the milk on the table and then laid Rose in her bed by the hearth. She started to cry, so he jiggled her cradle as Ellie moved a fry pan to the stovetop and cracked several eggs into it. She glanced at the bacon. "You cooked."

"I was hungry and bacon's about all I can cook."

"You didn't burn it." The eggs sizzled as the whites hardened. She flipped them over with a spatula.

Nick picked up Rose and held her in his arms, talking softly into her ear. The child's eyes widened with interest.

If anyone were to ride up to the cabin, they'd have thought the threesome a normal family.

Normal.

Ellie almost laughed at the thought. Nothing about her life had been normal, including this current situation.

"I'll protect you from Frank. And when he's captured, I'll leave you in peace."

A bitter taste settled in her mouth. "Don't make me any promises, Nick. They don't mean much to me. I've seen too many broken."

"I never break my promises."

She snorted.

He stared at her for what seemed an eternity. "I guess I'm just going to have to prove myself to you."

BY THE TIME they'd cleared the breakfast dishes, dark clouds had covered the blue sky and the wind had increased.

Nick set the freshly dried dishes on the counter by the washbasin. "The horses are in the barn. I'd best get them outside so they don't hurt themselves."

"Aren't they better off inside? They won't like the rain."

"Rain won't hurt them. But if they get spooked by the thunder while they are confined in their stalls, they could injure themselves."

Nick moved to the door and opened it. The breeze flapped the folds of his shirt. He reached for his duster, which now hung on the peg by the door.

Wiping her hands on her apron, Ellie glanced down at the sleeping infant and then hurried to the door. The whinnies of the horses drifted with the wind. The brewing storm had the animals' nerves dancing.

She didn't like dealing with horses. Their size intimidated her and she simply didn't understand them. Annie had said they all had their own personalities, but Ellie had decided if that were true, they were all stuck up and they didn't like her. None ever seemed to do what she wanted.

"I will get the horses," she said. "You could easily injure yourself."

"I've been around horses all my life."

"You've a gunshot wound in your leg that's only just started to heal. It won't take much to tear it open."

"I'll manage." He held out his duster. "But you take my coat. The skies are about to open up."

She hesitated. She considered arguing, then dismissed the idea. The man was stubborn, and worry over the horses and the storm drained the fight from her.

Ellie slid her arms into his coat. It smelled of him—earthy and masculine—and it engulfed her. "Nick, I will trip and fall if I wear this coat."

"Let me help. The coat will keep you dry." Efficiently he rolled up the sleeves.

He towered over her and the warmth from his body pulled her closer. She wanted to lean into him, to tell him to wrap his arms around her. Instead she held her breath, staring up at him.

As if sensing her gaze on him, he looked down. For a moment they stood there, unable to move.

A crack of thunder exploded outside. Seconds later, lightning sliced across the sky. Ellie jumped.

"Let's get the horses outside," he said.

Hugging her arms around her chest, she followed Nick toward the corral. Her skirts whipped around her ankles and her hair quickly escaped its topknot. Fat droplets of rain started to fall. Thunder cracked again in the distance.

Nick strode to the barn. It wouldn't take much to rip the stitches that weren't due to come out for another two days. Yet he didn't seem to care as he went inside the barn.

Ellie unlatched the gate and opened it. Nick emerged with two horses. His black mare, Aurora, pranced and bobbed her head, but she stayed steady as Nick guided the animal past Ellie and into the corral. He turned the mare and a gelding named Timmy loose and hurried back outside the fence. She closed the gate.

Thunder boomed over their heads. "I'll bring the others," Nick shouted. More lightning sliced the sky.

Nick emerged with more horses. Ellie took the reins of the first, a gelding called Brown Spots, as Nick turned the other, Joey, loose in the corral. Brown Spots pulled at his reins, nearly knocking Ellie over.

"Settle down," Nick shouted to Brown Spots. The animal quieted immediately.

"Yeah, he's good at ordering folks around," Ellie said to the horse.

The raindrops pinged faster against the earth. Soon, the rain was coming down in sheets and the dry earth quickly became mud. The water beaded on Nick's coat, but mud quickly coated Ellie's boots and the hem of her dress.

Nick let Brown Spots loose. Ellie, knowing they had little time, headed to the barn to get the remaining horse—Onyx, who was skittish on the best of days. Onyx left his stall with no trouble, but when they got outside in the wind and rain, he pawed at the dirt. Of all the horses, she liked him the least. And he felt the same about her.

Ellie tugged at the noose around Onyx's neck. "Do us both a favor and follow me to the corral without giving me trouble."

Rain had her eyes narrowing as she guided the horse to the corral. Ellie had nearly reached the gate when thunder clapped.

The horse reared, desperate to get free. Ellie would have let the animal go, uncaring if she ever saw it again, but Annie had taken a liking to Onyx.

The muscles in her arms tightened as she struggled to hold on to the rope. Her grip slipped. Her foot caught on the hem of Nick's coat and she lost her footing. She went down to her knees. Fearing the horse would crush her skull with his hooves, she struggled to stand.

Nick pushed her hand aside and, with a jerk of the rope, commanded the horse to stand still. It did. "Are you all right?"

"Yes."

He led the horse inside the corral. She slipped a second time before she managed to stand and head toward the porch at the same time as Nick.

The fabric of Nick's shirt clung to his body, exaggerating his broad shoulders and large arms. He took her breath away.

The rain had not enhanced her appearance, however. She was drenched and coated in mud.

"You have a tub?" he asked.

She tried to brush the mud from her skirt but only managed to smear it more. "There's one out back hanging on the wall," she said absently.

"I'll fetch it. You're a mess."

She lifted her chin. "I'm not afraid of a little dirt."

"You'll catch your death if you don't get warm and put on dry clothes." As if to demonstrate, he unbuttoned his shirt, shrugged out of it and hung it on a chair.

"I'll be fine." She didn't want to change into the dress Annie had given her. It was far too fine for everyday chores.

"Damn, woman, but you are stubborn." Without waiting for her, he retrieved the tub and set it in the kitchen by the stove. He returned with a large pot from the stove and then set it out in the rain. It quickly filled and he brought it back inside.

Panic flickered in Ellie. "I'm not stripping down and bathing with you in the house."

"I'll stay outside and give you all the privacy you need. I give you my word."

"Your word. What good is that to me?"

He lifted the pot full of rainwater and set it on the stove. "Now is as good a time as any for you to learn that you can trust me."

Gooseflesh puckered Ellie's chilled skin as her gaze dipped to his bare chest. The thought that he'd be even within shouting distance of her while she undressed seemed too much to consider. "No."

He leaned forward a fraction. "Suit yourself, but when you get sick, and you will, then I'm going to have to strip you down myself, wash you off and put you into bed."

Her heart pounded against her ribs.

"And," he added, "I will have to take care of Rose. I'll feed her and keep her changed, but I don't know anything about really mothering a child."

Her indignation softened a fraction. "A little mud and water aren't going to make me sick." She tried to speak with confidence, but he'd hit a nerve.

Nick found a towel and dried his black hair. He went to his saddlebag, pulled out a clean shirt and within minutes looked as if he'd never tussled with a couple of horses in the rain.

She probably looked like a rat that had been dragged out of a flooded mine shaft.

Ellie sighed. She was being foolish. If she did catch a chill and got sick, Rose wouldn't have anybody. "Fine."

Nick shrugged. "You're not doing me any favors."

She sat on the crate by the front door, unlaced her boots and set them side-by-side next to the door. She peeled off her wet stockings. Her skin puckered with the damp cold.

The idea of a hot bath tempted her so.

"Do you have anything else to wear?" he said. He set another pot out in the rain to collect more water.

"Annie gave me a dress." She'd never put on the store-bought garment. There'd been enough times she'd touched the fabric and dreamed of wearing the dress, but the occasion had never seemed special enough.

She went inside to the trunk at the base of her bed and opened it. She pulled out the simple blue calico. The material felt soft and the fabric smelled clean and fresh instead of like bacon grease and biscuits.

Nick set the second pot of rainwater on the stove. It would take a half hour before the two pots were fully heated—time enough to brush the tangles from her hair.

From the chest, she dug out the ivory comb Annie had given her and then sat by the stove, soaking up the warmth into her chilled skin. She started with the ends of her hair, knowing it would take her a good half hour to work her way up through the tangles.

Lord, if she'd only been blessed with straight hair, her life would have been a dozen times easier.

Nick sat with his book and opened it. He turned a page and her gaze was drawn to his long fingers. His sleeves were rolled up to his elbows, exposing the dark hair of his forearms.

A strange warmth spread from her belly through her limbs. Just looking at this man put her senses on alert.

This was bad. Very bad.

FRANK HUDDLED under a horse blanket as the rain pelted him. They way he figured it, he was about five days from the town of Thunder Canyon. There he'd get some real grub and find out if anyone had seen Ellie. The good thing about that red hair of hers was that folks rarely forgot it. He sure hadn't.

Water dripped from his nose and he shifted, burrowing deeper under the blanket. He'd been on the move since the night he'd shot Monty and he was getting damn tired of the hard living and the loneliness.

And the truth was, he missed Monty. Since they was kids, they'd been two peas in a pod. There'd been many nights that he sorely regretted killing him. If he hadn't been so mad, he might not have shot him. But when he'd found out that Jade and Monty had run off with the gold, he'd gone a little crazy.

Now his temper had cooled. And he knew deep down Monty wasn't bad. He was just a fool. Nothing had been right since Monty had met Jade. Jade had figured out what he'd liked and from then on had led him around by his Johnson. "Poor, dumb clod," Frank muttered. He hugged his blanket tighter.

Fact was, it was his fault Monty had met Jade. He'd been the one who had insisted they stop by the Silver Slipper when they were in Butte. Frank had a fondness for the redhead who'd worked in the kitchens. He'd never had the nerve to talk to her, but he liked being close to her. Her lily-white arms and the freckles on her nose warmed his heart. He liked it especially when she cooked those apple pies in the fall. He could close his eyes and imagine just for a moment that he was home in Missouri. In those days, his mama and pop were still well, and life was simple and clean.

Monty had met Jade at the Silver Slipper. And from the moment she'd got her hooks into him, it had been all downhill.

And now he was alone.

A cold chill shuddered down Frank's spine.

He closed his eyes and pictured Ellie. She had eyes as green as moss, though you had to look close to see them. She always kept her head down. Though she didn't talk much, he'd heard her speak to Adeline. Her voice had been as clear as church bells.

The night he'd shot Monty, there'd been terror in her eyes and he knew he'd been the one to put the fear in her. That, he regretted. She had a good, clean heart and he hated exposing her to such evil.

But he intended to make it all right between them. Ellie deserved better than the Silver Slipper and he aimed to see she got the better things in life.

Once he found Ellie, everything would be all right. He knew deep in his bones that his Ellie was the key to the gold. She'd been holding Monty's baby—his own flesh and blood—and she'd been the last to see Jade.

Frank didn't blame her for running. She'd been scared.

But once he found her, he'd explain everything. And once he had his gold, he'd have the means to ask for her hand in marriage. Together, they could raise Monty's baby.

He'd have his family back.

CHAPTER EIGHT

ELLIE SAT on the kitchen chair, her eyes closed, still combing tangles from her wavy hair. Every nerve in her body tingled at the thought of bathing with Nick so near.

She dreamed of him working the suds into her hair and over her skin. She thought about the feel of his lips against hers. The touch of his fingertips against her skin.

Her eyes snapped open. She was acting like a fool.

How many times had she vowed never, ever, to fall for a man like Nick Baron? A million? Two million?

Nick Baron's breed of man lived by his own rules. He was driven by private demons and he did what suited him best. If she let him into her heart, he'd use her and toss her aside.

Annie's man Mike was a rare breed: a good fellow. He showed his love for Annie in a million different ways—a touch, a look, a smile. He brought her candy from town. His gaze lingered on her when she wasn't looking.

Nick Baron had offered Ellie money for an hour in bed. And she'd be wise to remember that the next time she started dreaming about him touching her.

"Water's ready," he said.

His raspy voice startled Ellie. She glanced into the kitchen and realized Nick had lifted one of the steaming pots from the stove and had started to pour its contents into the tub. The muscles in his forearms were taut.

Her pulse thrummed at her wrists as she thought about those arms around her. She swallowed, shocked by her own weakness.

She stood quickly. "I can take care of the bath from here."

His eyes gleamed. "I'll finish it up. Just let me mix in some cold rainwater and then you'll be set."

Her mouth went dry. "Thanks."

When he'd poured the water into the tub and mixed it with his hands, he looked up at her. "Need any help getting undressed?"

The image of his hands soaping her naked back returned. "No!"

The edge of his mouth rose as if he were picturing the same scene. "Just offering." He moved toward the door. "If you change your mind, I'll be outside."

"I won't change my mind."

He chuckled.

THE RAIN CONTINUED to come down heavy and hard, trapping Nick outside on the porch. And as he listened to Ellie's wet dress hit the floor, he knew the true meaning of hell. He'd said he'd stay out on the porch and give her privacy, and he'd keep his word. Even if it killed him.

But no promise could stop his mind from wandering in erotic directions.

He leaned back and closed his eyes. Ellie's skin would be pale as porcelain and he imagined the freckles on the bridge of her nose spread all over her body. A man could spend a good deal of time counting and kissing each and every one of those freckles.

Her rosy-tipped breasts would skim the surface of the water as she lathered soap over her lean arms. Her waist would be trim and her hips and bottom gently rounded. He remembered with excruciating clarity what it had felt like to drape his hand over that waist.

Her prim-and-proper attitude didn't fit his image

of a sporting girl. She may have had sex, but he wondered if Ellie had ever known pleasure in a man's arms. If she'd ever moaned when her breasts were kissed or her body stroked.

Nick's body hardened and he stood. He strode toward the edge of the porch and stared out over the distant mountains. He'd gotten himself into one hell of a mess.

Through the open front door, he heard the baby coo and giggle. Curious, he moved into the house a few steps. He stopped when he glimpsed Ellie's naked back. She'd gotten the baby from her cradle and brought her into the bath with her. Drawn by the scene, he moved to the right to get a better look. Ellie cradled the child's wobbly head as she dipped her little body in the water. The baby grinned and kicked.

The sight took his breath away. And for a moment his chest ached. He thought of Crystal and the baby she'd borne. How old would the child be now? Nine? Ten?

When he and Crystal had married, they'd wanted a baby so much. They'd lain awake at night dreaming of their children, naming them and imagining what they'd do with their lives.

Nick shoved his hands into his pockets and turned. Lightning cracked across the sky. He cursed the rain that kept him bound so close to Ellie. The woman stirred things in him he'd long thought dead and buried with Crystal. And he didn't like it one bit.

He thought about his book sitting by the hearth. He'd have liked to have it now so that he could lose himself in the pages. But that would mean going back into the cabin, and he'd promised not to.

Nick closed his eyes and pulled in a deep breath. "Come on, Frank. Hurry up so we can get this over with."

Watching the pelting rain turn the dry dust to mud, he lost track of time.

"I'm finished," Ellie said from inside the house.

Nick turned and went into the house, annoyed he was so anxious to see her.

She laid the baby in the cradle by the hearth. As she straightened, he could see she'd put on a blue calico that, unlike the sack she'd worn before, hugged her breasts and very narrow waist. The blue dress was an inch or two shorter, too, leaving her trim ankles and bare feet exposed.

Stunned into silence, Nick's gaze slid up and down her body and settled on her face. She'd brushed her wet hair back and tied it with a strip of rawhide. Already it was beginning to curl. With her hair smoothed back, her high cheekbones, full lips and green eyes jumped out at him. The effect was devastating. No longer did she look like a scruffy girl, but a woman who could hold her own.

"Must feel good to get the grit off your skin." His voice sounded very rough.

Her skin glowed, as if she were embarrassed by his staring. "Yes."

"Annie gave you the dress?" He wished now she'd stayed in the old one. Its shapeless form hid her figure well. Before, putting her out of his mind had been tough; now, it would be nearly impossible.

"She bought it in town to wear to her brother's wedding but hasn't worn it since."

"Suits you well."

He would like to strip the dress off her right now. He didn't want to imagine the shapely body underneath, he wanted to see it.

His appraisal clearly put her on edge. Her back was as straight as a board and he could see she wasn't comfortable. If he acted on the primitive emotions pumping in his veins now, he imagined she'd jump right out of her skin.

And he didn't want her tense and worried when he touched her.

When he touched her.

Nick realized he would be touching her very soon. When this mess with Frank was over, he'd take her to his bed and he'd spend several days touching her.

Hell, who was he kidding? He could spend a lifetime with her and never get tired of it.

"You're staring," Ellie said. "Is something wrong?"

"No, nothing's wrong." He turned on his heel and walked back outside into the rain.

ELLIE WATCHED Nick step off the porch into the cold rain. He tipped his head briefly toward the heavens, as if savoring the cold.

"What are you doing?" she shouted.

"I'm going to check on the horses," he said, straightening.

"But we just put them out."

"This kind of storm could spook 'em," he called back. "I better go check."

He strode toward the corral.

Ellie wasn't sure what had just happened but she got the sense that she'd said or done something to make Nick mad. "Honestly, a woman could drive herself crazy trying to figure out a man like that," she muttered.

She glanced down at the baby, who lay in the cradle, bundled in a blanket. "Rose, men are a lot of work and I am not so sure they are worth the trouble."

The baby gurgled.

Ellie moved to the calendar pinned to the wall by the stove. Taking the pencil that hung on a string by it, she marked off the days since Annie had left. Seven. Lord, had it only been seven days? And still she had two, maybe three weeks before Annie returned. She wasn't sure if she would make it. The days were long enough as it was. And now, lying handcuffed to Nick would make the nights even longer.

Chores. She had enough chores to choke a horse and she had little time to be worrying over Nick Baron.

Ellie set to work and kept herself busy in the cabin for the next hour until the rain stopped. Anxious to get outside, she decided to collect the eggs from the henhouse. She'd missed yesterday and knew the nests would be full. She rigged a sling to hold the baby across her chest and, with an egg basket in hand, headed out the front door toward the chicken coop.

The afternoon sun peeked out through the thinning clouds. Storms could be violent out here, but they always seemed to go so quickly.

The wind flapped her skirts as she made her way through the mud. She glanced toward the barn, grateful that Nick wasn't underfoot. Thinking could be hard with him close and his sharp eyes seeming to read her mind.

She moved into the small, dark chicken coop, pausing until her eyes adjusted to the light. The dozen chickens clucked, each in a cubby built into the wall.

A brown hen pecked her hand and she reached for an egg. "Don't you flap your wings at me, old girl. I'm just here to collect a few eggs."

Ellie moved down the row, amazed at how efficient she'd become at the new tasks. In the city, there'd been no horses to tend or chicken coops to manage. Butte had just about anything she needed. When she'd arrived at the coach stop, she'd not known how to do much more than cook.

The dim room suddenly went almost pitch-black. She whirled around and in the doorway stood Nick. His broad shoulders all but blocking out the bright sun.

"Didn't you hear me calling?" he asked.

She shrugged. "No. With the wind howling outside the coop, I usually don't hear much. That's why I always take the baby with me."

"When you're finished, come back inside. We need to talk."

"About what?"

"When you're done, come inside."

Before she could question him further, he was gone.

By the time Ellie collected the eggs and returned to the cabin, her mind had rattled off a hundred different topics he might want to discuss. Was his wound bothering him? Had he changed his mind about keeping her here?

Ellie set her basketful of eggs on the table.

Nick stood next to the sink, a cup of water gripped in his hand. His expression was so dark and intense, her stomach tumbled.

She pulled the baby out of the sling and laid her in her cradle. "What's the matter with you?"

He shoved out a breath. "I thought you'd left."

She rolled her eyes. "How far do you think I'd have made it without a horse? You were in the barn with them."

He sighed, the logic of her words seemingly taking the wind out of his sails. "You could have walked."

"You're grasping now, mister. I wouldn't make it five miles with a baby in tow and no horse."

He gulped down the water and set the tin mug down. He seemed to struggle with his words. "Look, I know you don't want to be a part of this, but like it or not, you are."

"That I understand."

"The reward for Frank is one thousand dollars."

Her jaw dropped before she snapped it closed. That was more money than she'd see in a lifetime. "A fortune by any standards."

Her tone sparked annoyance in his eyes. "I'm not

chasing him for the money. I've got more than enough money saved up."

"What are you getting at?"

"If you'll agree to stay willingly, I'll give you the reward."

"You'll give me *one thousand dollars* if I don't run?" She laughed. "And I've a gold mine in Butte I can sell you for ten dollars."

He didn't look amused. "I could continue to hand-cuff us together at night to make sure you don't run, but I don't think either one of us wants that."

The memory of his hard body spooned against her buttocks last night had her blushing. She'd never been tempted to give herself to a man until last night. Spending another night beside him would not be wise. "No one gives away a thousand dollars."

"Some might, especially if they were worth a hundred times that."

She blinked. "You don't look like you have two nickels to rub together."

"I'm worth a lot of nickels."

She shook her head, trying to absorb the information. "Why do you want Frank so bad?"

He straightened his shoulders. "A friend of mine, Sheriff Bobby Pool, was one of the men guarding the gold when Frank and Monty hit the train. Frank killed him."

"How do I know all this is true? You could be working with Frank."

"I'm not. I want to see him behind bars."

His gaze was direct, unwavering and for some reason she believed him. "How do I know you are good for the money?"

"I'm good for it."

"How do I *know* that?"

White teeth flashed. "You're about the most untrusting female I've ever met."

"Miss Adeline's number one rule—never do anything for any man until you get paid first."

He worked his jaw. "The closest town is Thunder Canyon. After I capture Frank, I'll wire the marshal in Butte and have your money sent."

"You could run out on me and not pay."

"I've given you my word," he said slowly, as if speaking to a child. "And at night you won't be handcuffed to me, so I'm going to have to trust that you won't run."

True. This was an act of faith on his part, as well. The idea of getting one thousand whole dollars boggled her mind. "Why are you making me this offer? You don't have to."

"Like I said, you would be helping me and I don't need the money. You and Rose could use it."

"I want to keep Rose safe."

"I will let nothing happen to her, I swear it."

She believed he would protect Rose with his life. And still, she didn't want to believe his offer was true. "You don't really know us. Why give us so much money?"

"You saved my life."

Not good enough. "I *shot* you."

"And you could have butchered the hell out of me while you were digging those pellets out, but you didn't." He sighed. "I want to see that you and Rose are taken care of."

Silent, she stared at him, as if somehow she'd be able to peek inside his brain and see what he was thinking.

"One thousand dollars is a lot of reason to stay," Nick coaxed.

"It surely is." She paused and asked the question foremost in her mind. "What would I have to *do* for this money?"

"Just stay here and go about your days as you normally would. It won't take long for Frank to figure out where he can find his gold."

"But I don't know where the gold is!"

"He doesn't know that."

She hesitated. She realized for the first time that Nick believed her about the gold. A part of her heart softened. "You really believe me about the gold?"

His gaze held hers. "Yes."

For an instant she thought she might cry. She gazed out the window at the sunshine.

Nick stepped toward her. "Think of all the dresses you could buy for yourself and Rose."

Ellie laughed at such a silly notion. She faced him. "I'm not wasting my thousand dollars on dresses."

He cocked an eyebrow. "I've never known a woman who didn't like pretty things. What would you spend the money on if not dresses?"

She didn't have to think about her answer. "I'd give half to Annie right off the top. Lord knows where Rose and I would be if not for her. And with the balance, I'd move into Thunder Canyon. I'd open a café."

He stared at her with sharp interest. "A café in Thunder Canyon. Why would you leave here?"

"Annie's got a beau named Mike. He'll be offering for her hand soon, if I don't miss my guess. A newly married couple doesn't need Rose and me hanging around. They'll need their privacy and we'll need to make a permanent home for ourselves."

"Wouldn't it be easier to marry than to open a business?"

Typical man. She laughed. "If I'm going to break my back working each day, I'll keep the profits for myself."

He straightened. "So you accept my deal? Work with me and you're one thousand dollars richer."

She nibbled her bottom lip. "I feel as if I'm bargaining with the devil."

He laughed. "I've been called worse."

One thousand dollars was a fortune. And she didn't have to sell her body. *One thousand dollars*. It was just the start she needed to change her life. "All right, I'll take a chance on you."

He held out his hand. "Shake on it."

She hesitated, staring at his long fingers. She'd have been happy not to touch him at all because, honestly, she didn't trust herself one bit. But the challenge that sparked in his eyes prodded her to raise her hand and clasp his.

His large hand swallowed her small fingers. He squeezed her hand, shaking once. A jolt of energy shot up her arm. Her breath grew shallow and her pulse thrummed so loudly in her chest it was a wonder Nick didn't hear it. "And all I have to do is just wait with you? Nothing more?"

"Nothing more." He grinned. "Unless you *want* something more."

She snatched her hand back as if she'd been scalded. "Oh, no, all I want is the money."

He laughed. "A woman after my own heart. Deal?"

"Deal."

CHAPTER NINE

THE SUN had set. Ellie had cleaned the kitchen and fed Rose. Nick sat in one of the twin rockers near the hearth. Lantern light glowed, creating shadows on the whitewashed walls.

Ellie took her knitting box and sat in the empty rocker across from Nick. She was making a sweater for Rose.

This was the quiet time of day when the hard chores were done and she could sit by the fire for an hour or so before she climbed into bed. Most nights she did light mending, knitted or played checkers with Annie.

However tonight, as she sat across from Nick, a sudden restlessness took root, spreading through her. And the edginess had nothing to do with the prospect of the one thousand dollars.

He stared at his book, seemingly lost in its pages. Yet she was very aware of the way his long fingers cupped the soft leather, the rise and fall of his chest and the hair that curled in the V of his shirt, buttoned up to within inches of his collarbone.

Ellie dropped a stitch. Cursing her clumsiness, she recaptured the yarn on the needle. She finished the row but found tracking the stitches a struggle.

She glanced at Nick. He wasn't reading. He was staring at her. Unrepentant, he lowered his gaze back to the pages.

Quickly she returned her focus to her knitting. Her heart pounded in her chest. She dropped another stitch and recovered it only to let it slip again.

She peeked at Nick again. She realized then that he'd not turned any pages. Neither of them could concentrate.

Struggling to fill the silence that only stoked her restlessness, she said, "Do you read every night?"

Nick's blue eyes looked into hers. "Just about."

His attention made her mouth feel as dry as the desert. "What do you read?"

"See for yourself." He closed the book and handed it to her.

She set her knitting down and accepted the book. His fingers brushed hers. Her pulse tripped.

The book's binding was smooth and fine. She thumbed through the pages, trying to hide the quake in her fingers. The letters were very, very small. "What's it about?"

"A famous general."

She closed the book and handed it back to him. Their fingers touched again and a frizzle of energy shot up her arm. Her cheeks burned. "It's a fine-looking book, just like the other one."

He cocked an eyebrow.

She shrugged. "Remember, I went through your saddlebag when you were unconscious."

"Ah, I forgot."

He didn't seem angry, so she continued. "The other one is written in a different language."

"That book is written in Latin."

She started to knit a new row. "What's that?"

"It's a dead language, spoken by people who lived long ago."

She shook her head as she knitted a few more stitches. "Why would anyone care about a language no one speaks anymore?"

"The ancient teachers had much to offer."

Ellie stared at him as if he'd grown a third eye. "You're a puzzle to me, Nick Baron. You look meaner than any outlaw I've ever seen and yet you read better than the smartest teacher in Butte." The question that had plagued her since the moment she'd found the photo welled inside her. "Is it because Crystal and your baby died?"

A smile tugged at the edge of his mouth. "Always direct."

"Best way to be if you want folks to know what you're after."

For a moment he was silent and she thought perhaps he'd forgotten her question. Then he seemed to come to a decision. "I had trouble with the law back East."

"Can't say I'm surprised."

He lifted his chin. "It wasn't all my fault."

She met his gaze. "It never is."

To her surprise, he laughed. *"Touché."*

"What happened?"

His smile faded, replaced by a look of acceptance and resolve. "I nearly beat my older brother Gregory to death. I was charged with attempted murder." His voice was edged in steel.

"Why?" she said, her voice as soft as a prayer.

He set his book down on the small side table by his rocker. "We competed constantly when we were growing up. Gregory's mother was my father's first wife. When she died and Father remarried my mother, Gregory never felt as if he belonged and he resented me and the attention my father gave me."

"That's not your fault."

"Don't fool yourself, I was just as competitive as he was. In my younger days, I had a need to best him in everything. When he joined the army, I had to do the same. The rivalry between us grew ugly when I started to rise through the ranks faster than he did. Gregory started drinking and his drunkenness ended up getting him court-martialed. He returned home bitter and angry. His drinking didn't improve and then our father changed his will. He left the lion's share of the family lands to me and our sister Julia instead of Gregory. It wasn't personal. Father knew Gregory would never be happy managing the lands, whereas I would gladly return after my military service ended."

He tapped his long finger on the armrest of the rocker. "Soon after Father's announcement, I was stationed in Kansas. The territory was dangerous and the Indian wars at their height. Crystal stayed behind in Virginia." His eyes darkened. "While I was gone, Gregory seduced my wife. She became pregnant. I returned home almost a year to the day from when I'd left. She'd died the day before, giving birth."

"How did you know it was Gregory?"

"I found Crystal's diary. She confessed the affair and her plans to send the child away before I returned. I got blinding drunk and went after him."

"You sound so calm when you talk about this."

A raw intensity radiated from his body. "Don't be

fooled. There was a time when the anger burned so fierce it nearly consumed me. I'd have gladly killed Gregory if my sister Julia hadn't stumbled upon us and begged me to see reason."

"You said you had trouble with the law."

"Gregory recovered and pressed charges. He'd have seen me rot in jail if my father hadn't interceded. The charges were dropped on the condition I never return to Virginia. In the end Gregory got what he wanted—his inheritance."

"And so you came West?"

"I was a soldier and good at hunting men. When I arrived in Denver, there was a reward posted for a man wanted for stealing. I tracked him down and brought him in to the authorities. I collected the reward. It seemed a good way to make money, so I followed the trail of another wanted man. He led me to Montana. Ever since, there's always been someone new to track."

"Sounds like you've led an interesting life. You've seen so many places. All I've ever seen is Butte and the Spring Rock station."

"I am not that interesting. In fact, I am a bit of a cliché."

"Cliché? What's that?"

"A story everyone has heard a thousand times. The solider cuckolded by his wife."

"You're not the first man and you won't be the last."

"It will never happen to me again. I will never let a woman twist me around her finger like Crystal did."

A long silence stretched between them. "Why did you tell me all this?" she said.

"I don't want there to be any secrets or surprises between us when we make love."

Her mouth dropped open. She snapped it closed, amazed at his arrogance. "How do you know we *even* are?"

"I know."

"I'm not the least bit interested in you."

"Yes, you are," he said, a ghost of a smile touching his lips.

"This is insane." She rose, feeling suddenly warm. "I'm going to bed."

"Want company?"

"No!" She ran to her room and closed the door. But instead of going to bed, she pressed her ear against the door, listening for any signs that he had followed her.

His purposeful footsteps crossed the main room. They paused in front of her door and then, after a long moment, started up the stairs toward the second-floor room he'd claimed.

She squeezed her eyes shut. To her amazement, she realized she was disappointed he hadn't knocked on her door.

ELLIE SHOULD HAVE BEEN exhausted when she climbed into her own bed that night. But she wasn't. Worries about Nick twisted inside her. The ceiling above her head creaked with his footsteps as he paced. He couldn't sleep, either.

She rolled onto her back and stared up at the plank ceiling. It struck her then that she *wanted* Nick with a power so fierce it rattled her like a bucking bronco.

Ellie had never been with a man before, but she wasn't a prissy miss, either. She knew what a man and woman did in bed. And she knew it wasn't always about business for the women. She'd heard the girls giggling and whispering about what they'd done.

She'd never felt any desire for a man before. And she'd come to believe she was immune to such feelings—which had always been just fine. She didn't want to be like her mother and the other women at the Silver Slipper.

But this desire for Nick was singing in her veins. It was changing her—making her want things she'd never wanted before. The change frightened her.

Ellie rolled onto her side and stared at the patches

of her quilt. She considered counting each of the tiny stitches that surrounded each square. She sighed. It would be hours before sleep came. She rolled onto her back.

A crash outside had her sitting up in bed. Suddenly her heart was pounding in her chest. She tossed back the covers and sprang out of bed.

Nick's footsteps pounded down the stairs as she lit a lantern and hurried into the center of the cabin.

Nick had strapped on his holster and was checking the bullets in the chamber of his gun.

"Do you think it's Frank?"

Lantern light glowed on the hard edges of his face. "I don't know. Kill that light."

Ellie blew out the flame. The darkness surrounded them. "I wasn't expecting him this soon."

"I was."

He strode across the cabin as if it were the middle of the day. He pushed back the red-checked curtain with the tip of his pistol, allowing moonlight to shine inside the cabin.

Ellie stepped forward. Her hip bumped into the corner of the kitchen table. She winced and set her lantern down on the table. "Can you see anything?"

"No."

"Should I get my gun?" she said.

"No!"

Nerves had her chattering. "I would think Frank wouldn't make so much noise. Are you sure it's not an animal?"

He sighed. "All I can hear right now is you talking."

"Sorry."

Nick stared out the window. Time dragged. Finally he stood and took the latch off the front door.

"Where are you going?"

"To greet our visitor." He opened the door.

Shadows flitted across the front porch. A chill hovered in the air and a ring of mist circled the full moon.

Another crash to their right had Nick turning with lightning speed. He took a step outside and Ellie trailed behind, hovering close to him.

They peeked around to the side porch. Moonlight shone on a bear cub sitting in the bathtub on the front porch. The animal lay on its back, its overlarge paws thrust in the air. When it saw Nick, it scrambled out of the tub and ran off into the dark.

Nick straightened his shoulders, obviously relieved. He guided Ellie back inside. When the door was closed and latched, he holstered his gun. "Cubs can get into all kinds of mischief."

Ellie moved beside Nick and peered out the side window. Her nerves still hummed from the bear's unexpected arrival. "Annie said they are cute but dangerous. She said they can travel in pairs."

"With their mothers close by."

His warm breath brushed her skin. She couldn't move.

"Very fierce, no doubt," she said, exhaling, her voice traveling with her breath. Strength radiated from Nick's body. Ellie found it intoxicating to stand this close to him.

The excitement was over. They could have returned to their beds. But neither moved.

Her nipples hardened and pushed against the coarse fabric of her nightgown. She moistened her dry lips with her tongue. His scent enveloped her.

Drawn by an unseen force, Ellie looked up at him. He was staring down at her, his chiseled face barely visible in the moonlight. His lips looked full, inviting.

A small scar ran down the right side of his chin. Guided by unfulfilled desires, she traced the mark with the tip of her finger. His unshaven jaw scraped her skin. This simple touch thrilled her more than she could have imagined.

He tensed but didn't move away from her.

Her heart slammed against her chest. "How did you get that scar?"

"I was a young boy," his said, his voice a hoarse

whisper. "I snuck into my father's study to see his new dagger. I'd removed it from its sheath and was studying the tip when my father walked into the study. I jumped and cut myself."

She resisted the urge to touch his lips. "Was he angry?"

He captured her hand in his strong fingers. "Not when he saw all the blood gushing from the wound."

She edged a half step closer to him. "You carry a fine dagger in your saddlebag."

"It's the same one."

"Did you get into a lot of trouble when you were a boy?"

A small smile lifted the edges of his mouth. "No more than my share."

Her gaze settled on his lips. She wondered if he kissed her, whether the kiss would be chaste or demanding. She suspected the latter—Nick Baron wasn't a man who did anything halfway.

She didn't have to wait long for her answer.

As if he'd read her mind, he leaned his head forward and pressed his lips to hers. For a moment she stood very still, stunned by his touch. So gentle.

The tender kiss might have satisfied her curiosity, but it also stoked new, hotter fires inside her. She rose up on tiptoe and deepened the kiss.

Nick reacted immediately. He banded his arm

around her waist and pulled her to him. His hard chest pressed against her breasts. The stubble of his beard rubbed her chin. Every nerve in her body danced with a newfound vigor.

Their bodies molded together as if they'd been made for each other. Kissing him felt so good. Her body sang. Her head swam. She wanted *more* of him.

Ellie fisted handfuls of his shirt between her fingers. A soft mew escaped her throat. Even to her own ears, she sounded desperate and hungry.

Nick coaxed her lips open. His tongue explored her mouth, sending more waves of pleasure through her body. Heat burned at her core.

A savage noise rumbled in his chest. He broke the kiss. "I want you."

His voice was rougher than the jagged mountain peaks. Ellie couldn't speak.

This was all so wonderful.

And it felt very, very good.

The urge to surrender herself to him had her ready to say yes.

Then Nick whispered the things he wanted to do to her when he got her into bed. The raw language cut through the haze of desire. Shock radiated through her limbs. Her mind cleared. He'd spoken to her as though she was a whore. She felt dirty.

She pulled out of his arms. Her hands trembled as she pushed a mop of curls off her face.

Nick Baron stared down at her, his hooded eyes filled with dark desire. "What's wrong?"

"The way you spoke to me—I didn't like it." She sounded like a prissy schoolgirl.

He looked surprised. "I thought you'd like what I said."

The fire in her was gone. "I didn't."

He reached out to her as if desperate to return to what they'd had. "Then I won't say those things again. I promise to make it good for you."

He captured the thin folds of her sleeve in his fingertips. She pulled back. "No."

He released the fabric. "There is something between us, Ellie. I feel it and so do you. Why are you fighting it? There is no reason why we can't enjoy each other."

In all the years she'd lived in the brothel she'd protected the innocence inside her. She'd guarded it, believing the right man would cherish her. It shook her to her core to realize she'd nearly tossed away what she'd saved for so long. Adeline had always said some handsome man with smooth moves would steal away her purity and then, before she knew it, she'd be selling herself. She'd denied it and yet here she was.

A moment passed before she could speak in a

calm voice. "I'm sure it would be real nice, but you're not offering what I really want."

"What *do* you want?" His voice was ragged with desire.

She felt foolish now. "Marriage."

He looked shocked.

She shrugged. "And with marriage, I want a home."

He stepped back as if she'd tried to burn him. He rubbed the back of his hand over his mouth. "I can't give you that. After Crystal, I swore I'd never marry again."

She lifted her chin. "Somehow I'd expected that answer." She kept her voice even, but her insides felt twisted and bruised.

"I'm sorry."

"No need. Fact, it's good we both know where we stand now."

CHAPTER TEN

ELLIE TOSSED and turned most of the night, dreaming of Nick. She fed the baby around two but despite her exhaustion she couldn't fall back to sleep. An hour before dawn, she could stand it no more. Her sheets were twisted, her body ached and her eyes were puffy with fatigue. She climbed out of her bed, anxious for chores that would take her mind off Nick.

When Nick came downstairs an hour later, she had biscuits, fried ham and eggs on the table.

Nick grabbed a couple of biscuits and a cup of coffee. "I've got stalls to clean."

"Okay." She didn't protest or encourage him to eat. She needed distance from him.

Ellie moved to the window and watched him stride toward the barn. He walked with the confidence of a man comfortable in his abilities. He was a man who knew what he did and did not want.

And he didn't want marriage.

She sighed. There was no fretting over what just wasn't going to be.

Ellie did her best not to think about Nick. She cleaned the ashes from the stove, she dragged the kitchen rug outside and beat the dust from it, and she cared for Rose. Yet no matter how busy she was, her mind kept drifting back to him, to the look of raw passion burning in his eyes when he'd looked at her last night.

She also thought a lot about the things he'd whispered in her ear—the things he'd like to do to her—and she found she wasn't as shocked or repulsed as time passed. In fact, thinking about what he'd said sounded kind of fun.

Lord help her. And take Nick Baron out of her life before her resolve melted and she gave herself to him.

Ellie was churning butter on the porch when Nick strode out of the barn. His shirt was stained with sweat. Her heart jumped at the sight of him.

"There's cool water on the kitchen table," she said. "I reckon you're thirsty."

"Thanks." He disappeared into the house and returned moments later with a mug for himself and one for her. He handed her the glass.

She was touched he'd thought of her. "You didn't have to do that." She sipped her water. It was refreshing.

"Was no trouble." He rubbed his thigh.

"Is your wound bothering you? It's not infected, is it?"

"The stitches bother me. They itch."

"They should be ready to come out now." She didn't trust herself to touch him. "Give me about a half hour to finish the butter and then I'll have a look at them."

Nick nodded stiffly. She sensed he didn't like the idea of her touching him, either. But there was no getting around what had to be done.

Thirty minutes later Nick sat at the kitchen table, his bare legs covered with a blanket. His right leg, which looked as if it had been sculpted from granite, was exposed. Dark hair curled around the white bandage.

Butterflies fluttered in her stomach. What worried her more than anything was that she *wanted* to touch him.

She sighed. The sooner she got his stitches removed, the sooner he could get back to his chores. And maybe, just maybe, she'd get a lucky break and Frank would show very *soon,* Nick could catch him *soon,* she'd get her reward money *soon* and she could get on with her life!

"This shouldn't take but a minute," she said.

Nick sat with his hands fisted on his thighs as if

he were expecting a great deal of pain. He probably didn't like being partially clothed and vulnerable. "Fine."

Ellie set her medical box on the table. "Taking stitches out is painless. You don't have to worry."

He unfurled his fingers, joint by joint, until his palms rested at his sides. "I'm not worried about pain."

"Oh." Ellie retrieved the small scissors from the box and knelt beside him. "I'm going to cut away the bandage." She tucked a curl behind her ear and leaned closer to him. The heat of his body radiated around her as she slid the blade under the white muslin.

He didn't flinch but his breathing grew shallower. It was clear he didn't like having her close.

Ellie gently peeled off the bandage. To her great relief, the wound had puckered gently. There was no hint of redness or infection around the seven neat stitches. "The salves have worked nicely. You shouldn't even have much of a scar."

He nodded. "Just get the stitches out."

Ellie leaned closer and slid the scissors under the first stitch, snipped it and then gently tugged it free. She repeated the process six more times. "All out. Let me put a little salve on the wound and a small bandage and then you are done."

"Okay."

She grabbed the salve jar and dug out a liberal portion with her fingers. She smoothed it gently over the wound. His muscles felt hard under her fingertips. "It's a good idea to favor the leg for a few more days. You could still tear the wound open." The salve's aggressive scent filled the air around them.

He wrinkled his nose. "What is that? It smells like dung."

Ellie laughed. "They're herbs. I know they smell bad, but they really are quite effective. I smeared this stuff all up and down your leg when you were unconscious."

He turned his head. "It's a wonder I didn't die from the fumes."

"Consider yourself lucky. You *were* unconscious. I was awake."

He grunted.

She washed her hands. "The wound needs to be bandaged for a few more days."

"Fine."

She'd bandaged the leg a half dozen times over the last week, but with him sitting here glaring down at her, the moment just felt too intimate. She cleared her throat. "Stand up so I can wrap the bandage around your leg to protect it a couple more days."

He glanced down at the blanket. He'd have to expose more of himself so she could complete the task. "I can take it from here, Ellie. Just give me the bandage."

Grateful, she handed the clean strips of muslin to him. She turned her back, facing the sink to give him privacy.

He began to wrap his leg.

"Don't wrap it too tight," she said, her back to him. "It will cut off the flow of blood."

"Right."

Lord help her, but she itched to turn around and help him. "Are you sure you don't need help?"

"Positive."

The sound of wagon wheels rumbling into the front yard silenced her.

Muttering an oath, Nick finished wrapping the bandage and pulled on his pants. "Damn, you'd think this place was the only coach stop in Montana."

"It's the only one for a hundred miles." Ellie went to the front window and peeked outside. "It's one of the Starlight coaches. The driver is Sandy. He's one of our regular customers."

He strapped on his gun. "I will walk outside with you."

"I already told you, I recognize the driver."

"Do you know who is in his coach? Do you know

whether or not Frank is sitting inside the coach with a gun drawn, ready to shoot both of us?"

"I'd not thought of that."

"Until Frank is captured, you better start thinking like that. He is as mean as a snake and very, very cunning."

Ellie sighed.

"You put yourself in the middle of this mess when you ran with that baby," he said. His voice had lost the edge of anger.

Ellie straightened her shoulders. He was right. She'd made a choice. But she'd never take it back. Rose was worth the danger.

Managing a bright smile, Ellie pulled off her apron and smoothed the stray curls of her hair. "Lead the way."

NICK STRODE OUTSIDE. He kept Ellie behind him as he studied the face of Sandy, the driver. The man looked young. A spray of freckles covered the bridge of his nose and his body and blond beard had yet to fill out.

Sandy set the hand brake and hopped down off the driver's seat. The smile on his face vanished when he saw Nick. "Ellie, everything all right here?"

Ellie peeked around Nick. Her smile was radiant and so full of life. Nick felt a pang of jealousy as she pushed past him and walked up to the driver. She held out her hand. "It's fine, Sandy."

Sandy took her hand. "You're looking real fine today, Ellie." The boy was smitten with her.

She blushed. "Thank you."

"That a new dress?"

She ran her hands over the blue fabric. "Annie gave it to me. My other one is soaking. I took a little tumble in the mud."

Nick did not like the easy familiarity between the two. It grated on his nerves. His shoulder brushed hers as he held out his hand to Sandy. "My name is Nick Baron."

Sandy's eyes narrowed. "The bounty hunter."

The reputation that had worked so well for him in the past now haunted him. "That's right."

"You sure everything is all right here?" Sandy asked Ellie.

"Yes."

"Has he been here long?" Sandy asked.

"I am waiting on an old friend," Nick said. A part of him admired the young pup's grit. The boy reminded him of himself when he'd been young and in love.

"Well, your friend won't have any trouble finding Annie's coach stop," Sandy said to Nick. "Ellie's cooking has sparked new interest in the place."

"So I've discovered," Nick said.

Ellie took a small step away from Nick. "Any passengers today?"

Sandy's eyes widened as if he'd forgotten all about his passengers. "Sure are. Better let them out." He hurried to the side of the coach, opened the door and lowered the folding stairs. "We're here at Annie's, folks. Step right on out!"

The driver extended his hand into the coach and helped an older woman down. Dressed in black, she was short and portly. Her gray hair was tightly bound under her black, lace-trimmed bonnet.

"What a horrendous ride!" the woman said. "I've never known a coach driver to drive so fast."

"Mrs. Douglas, I wanted to get you here so you could sample some of Miss Ellie's fine cooking before we make the final push to Thunder Canyon." Sandy winked at Ellie. "Be right back—got to run to the necessary."

Mrs. Douglas dabbed a lace handkerchief to her lips. "My bones will ache for weeks."

Ellie moved to the carriage. "Welcome."

Mrs. Douglas's gaze slid up and down Ellie. She handed Ellie her small satchel. "Do you have honey this time? The last time we passed through, you didn't have honey. I can't enjoy my meal unless I have honey on my bread."

"We are well stocked," Ellie said. "And I have chokeberry preserves that I put up only last week."

Mrs. Douglas shook her head. "Stains my teeth. I want honey."

"Of course."

Nick didn't like the woman. He was tempted to put her back in the coach and to tell Sandy to keep driving.

A tall, thin man jumped down off the carriage. Black hair drooped over his clean-shaven face. He wore a gray wool suit and a hat made of beaver. He rubbed the back of his neck and turned his face toward the sun.

Ellie recognized him instantly. "Dr. Robert Morgan. You passed through about five weeks ago."

The doctor smiled as he looked at her. "Ah, Mrs. Watson! I was hoping to see you again."

Mrs. Watson. So, Ellie was passing herself off as a widow.

"Spring Rock and you are the bright spot on this very, very long trip," the doctor said, moving toward her. Despite the complaint, his tone was good-natured.

Ellie smiled. "Where's your horse, Dr. Morgan?"

He grinned. "She went lame in the last town. Sandy was kind enough to give me a ride back to Thunder Canyon."

Dr. Morgan removed his hat. "You're looking fit."

"You're looking well yourself." She nodded toward Nick. "This is Mr. Baron. He's also a guest."

Nick took the doctor's smooth, uncallused hand. "Dr. Morgan."

The carriage shifted as someone moved inside it. There was a loud thud and a woman's screech.

"I doubt I can endure another coach stop," a young woman complained. She peeked out the carriage door. Black ringlets dangled around a plump face.

"Only one to go before we are home, Robyn," Mrs. Douglas said as she brushed the dust from her sleeve. "Doctor, would you mind helping my daughter down from the carriage?" Her tone was overly sweet.

Dr. Morgan tore his gaze from Ellie and held out his hand to Miss Douglas, who was about Ellie's age.

"Come on, Miss Douglas, and stretch your legs," Dr. Morgan said.

Miss Douglas smiled at the doctor. "Thank you," she said, softening her tone. She placed her hand on his shoulder and leaned on him as she climbed down.

"Welcome," Ellie said.

Miss Douglas, who wore a stylish green traveling dress, didn't look at Ellie as she brushed the trail dust from her skirts.

Miss Douglas had been spoiled and protected all her life, Nick decided. He knew her type. Though she was about the same age as Ellie, he would bet Ellie possessed twice her wisdom and maturity.

Miss Douglas's glass-green gaze traveled around the small coach stop. "I don't like this place. It always looks so dirty."

Mrs. Douglas glanced down at her daughter and then smiled at the doctor. "Yes, well one must do what one must do."

"I liked the hotel in Denver better," Miss Douglas whined.

"We're not as fancy here," Ellie said brightly. "But the place is clean and the food is good."

"It's always a pleasure to visit," Dr. Morgan said.

"Where is Annie?" Mrs. Douglas asked.

"She's gone to see her folks. She'll be back before the snow falls."

"Annie knows how to take care of us," Mrs. Douglas said.

"I'm sure I can handle whatever you need."

"I want you to put Dr. Morgan's expenses on my tab today," Mrs. Douglas said.

"That's not necessary," Dr. Morgan said, blushing.

"Nonsense," the older woman replied.

He nodded. "Thank you for your generosity."

Nick shifted his stance, wincing. His leg ached and he found his patience growing thin.

The doctor noticed immediately. "An injury, Mr. Baron?"

"Gunshot wound."

Mrs. Douglas paled. "Oh, my. I hope it wasn't one of those desperate renegade *Indians?*"

Nick didn't like the emphasis she'd placed on "Indian." Though he'd fought many fierce battles against the Indians in Kansas, he'd learned to respect not only their fighting skills but their cultures. "No Indians."

"Then who?" Miss Douglas asked.

"An outraged redhead," Nick said.

The doctor glanced toward Ellie. "Mrs. Watson shot you?"

"That's right," Nick said.

She folded her arms over her chest as fire spit from her vibrant eyes. She wasn't pleased he'd mentioned the shooting.

Mrs. Douglas's shocked expression mirrored her daughter's. Their gazes moved to Ellie as if the news had shaken their notions of her. "My daughter and I are going inside to get out of the sun. Dr. Morgan, will you join us?"

"In a moment," he said.

The women scurried inside but Dr. Morgan

seemed in no rush to follow. His eyes filled with admiration and wonder as he stared at Ellie.

However, Ellie didn't seem to notice anyone but Nick. She looked as though she could shoot him again. "I doubt Mr. Baron will be sneaking up on my coach stop again."

Nick tugged the horse free of the harness. "Learned my lesson."

The doctor looked torn between amusement and concern. "I'd be glad to have a look at your wound, Mr. Baron."

Nick shrugged. "I feel fine."

"I'd like you to take a look at it just the same," Ellie said. "Always best to have a doctor double check."

Nick looked at her, surprised by her words. "Whatever the lady wants."

Ellie blushed and glanced away.

The doctor nodded. "Let me get my bag from the coach."

Forty-five minutes later the guests were settled inside with their meal. Nick had put up the horses and he and the doctor had gone to sit outside on the porch, where the doctor could inspect Nick's wound in privacy and with good light.

Ellie stayed inside. Nick knew she wanted to be outside, but she seemed worried that Mrs. Douglas wouldn't approve of her attending the examination. Ellie might have nursed Nick while he was ill and seen him in his wherewithal, but now that Mrs. Douglas and the others were here, the rules had changed. He felt a distance between them that he didn't like.

"Ellie," Nick called, knowing she hovered close.

Immediately she poked her head out the door. "Everything all right?"

"You can come out now," Nick said, fastening his belt buckle.

She stepped outside just as Nick strapped on his gun. The doctor, who had slung his coat over the porch railing during the examination, was rolling down his sleeves.

"So how did Mr. Baron fare?" Ellie asked.

Dr. Morgan fastened his cuffs. "You did a fine job with him, Mrs. Watson."

Nick could feel Ellie's gaze on him. "I've put an herb poultice on it every day," Ellie said. "He had a fever but it broke several days ago."

The doctor nodded. "I've a mixed mind about the homemade herb poultices. Some do more harm than good," he said.

She paled. "Did I harm Mr. Baron?"

"You mean, beyond shooting me?" Nick muttered.

Ellie glared at him.

"There's not the smallest sign of infection." The doctor looked at Nick. "Any pain?"

"Only when Ellie pokes at it," Nick said dryly. "Or when I stand too long."

The doctor nodded. "I'd say you're going to make a full recovery, Mr. Baron. Whatever Mrs. Watson put on the wound did the job. Fact, I'd like to know what was in that poultice."

Ellie sighed, relieved. "I'd be happy to give the recipe to you."

"Mrs. Watson!" Mrs. Douglas called. "I need you this instant."

Ellie glanced into the cabin. "Excuse me, gentlemen."

Nick watched Ellie scurry into the house. It annoyed him to see her waiting on people. She deserved better.

The doctor pulled on his coat. "I'd say you are one lucky man, Mr. Baron. A couple inches to the right and she could have hit an artery. I doubt anyone could have saved you then."

"I'll always be grateful for her terrible aim."

"Be grateful that Ellie is also such a fine nurse. This gal did a better job on you than a lot of doctors would have. If that fever was as bad as I think, she'd have had to have worked night and day to keep it under control."

"I have only vague memories of the fever. But I knew Ellie was always close."

"And all the while she had a baby to care for and she kept this stop running. The woman is nothing short of a miracle worker."

Aye, few women could match Ellie. "How long before I can ride?" he said, needing to change the subject.

"About a week."

"That's what Ellie said."

"She's a smart woman." The doctor stared into the house after Ellie. "The kind of gal that would suit a country doctor."

Nick's eyes narrowed. "You lost me."

"Mrs. Watson. She's a damn fine woman."

Nick sucked in a slow breath. "And?"

"I was thinking spring would be a fine time to court her."

Nick had no claims to Ellie. Still, the idea that the doctor wanted to court her ate at his gut. "You barely know her."

"She's a widow. She's got a fine heart and she loves that baby. Couldn't ask for better."

Nick ground his teeth. "I best see to hitching up the fresh team. I don't want to keep you all waiting."

"But I thought you were a guest here?" Dr. Morgan asked.

The doctor's sudden interest surprised him. "I have never been good at sitting and waiting. It is better that I work."

Dr. Morgan fell into step beside Nick. "Mind if I tag along? The Douglas women are charming but a little can go a long way."

"Suit yourself."

Nick opened the corral gate and looped a rope around two fresh mares.

"Something wrong, Mr. Baron?"

Nick shook his head. "Nope."

Dr. Morgan squinted against the bright sun. Already, the sun had burned his pale skin. "I saw the way Ellie worried over your wounds. She has an affection for you. Is there something between you two?"

Nick was silent for a moment. Ellie cared about him. The idea warmed his heart. But she wanted marriage and he couldn't give that. "No."

The doctor's shoulders relaxed. "Good. I don't wish to poach." He shoved his hands into his pockets, the worry lines from his brow vanishing. "I believe I am ready for lunch now." Whistling, he strode back to the cabin.

Nick clenched and unclenched his fingers. His life was unsettled and his future uncertain. He didn't know what he wanted or where he'd end up. He had no business wanting Ellie. Hell, he didn't know if he had the makings of a father.

Yet, inwardly, he crossed an invisible threshold. From now on, Ellie was off limits.

CHAPTER ELEVEN

MRS. DOUGLAS'S CHATTER drifted around Ellie as she stared out the front door wondering why Nick hadn't joined them for lunch. Dr. Morgan had said Nick was in the barn, checking on the horses.

But he'd been gone for nearly an hour.

Worry had crept into Ellie's bones. Horses could be such dangerous creatures. They could easily kill a man with one kick. What if Nick had had an accident with one of the horses?

Ellie caught herself. She had no business fretting over a man she had no claim to—a man who'd said his only interest in her was sexual. What was wrong with her? He'd told her marriage wasn't in the cards for him. He'd *told her* he'd leave as soon as Frank was caught. And yet, here she stood worrying over him.

Rose started to fuss and Ellie turned from the door. She went to the baby's cradle and picked her up. The child's cries slowed but she rooted around Ellie's breast and fussed.

Ellie made a bottle and chose a seat by the window to nurse. She glanced outside again toward the barn. She was being very, very silly now, but if Nick wasn't back in fifteen minutes, she would go find him.

Sandy tore off a large piece of bread and put it on his plate. "That baby is growing like a weed, Ellie."

The baby suckled the nipple as if she were half starved. She smiled down at her daughter. "She sure does eat a lot."

"Well, she is a cutie," Sandy said. "You ever seen such a pretty baby, Mrs. Douglas?"

The older woman barely glanced toward Ellie. "Of course. My Robyn was the prettiest baby there ever was." Mrs. Douglas returned to her conversation with the doctor, while Miss Douglas circled her fork around a half-eaten piece of cornbread.

Ellie had spent her life serving people and had grown to expect that customers would ignore her or treat her as if she were a piece of furniture. But she'd never gotten used to it or liked it.

Nick strode into the room. Ellie glanced up, surprised he'd reached the cabin without her seeing him. The man moved as silently and quickly as a cat.

Ellie started to rise. "Let me get you a plate, Mr. Baron."

He raised a brow as if amused by her sudden use

of his surname. "Sit, *Mrs.* Watson. I can make a plate for myself. You are feeding the baby."

"Mrs. Watson," Mrs. Douglas said, as if Nick hadn't spoken, "I'd like more butter for my bread." The butter crock was three feet from the older woman, on the counter behind her.

Standing, Ellie pulled the bottle out of the baby's mouth. Rose cried. She popped the nipple back in and started toward the stove.

Nick intercepted her. "Sit," he ordered.

Nick picked up the butter and set it down loudly in front of Mrs. Douglas. The older woman's gaze flicked up to his. The annoyance that sparked in her brown eyes vanished when she looked at him.

Sandy wiped his plate clean with a piece of bread. "I sure could use a piece of that pie I saw cooling in the window. I'll bet it's a chokeberry pie."

Nick looked as if he wanted to pull the coach driver out of his chair. "Get the piece yourself, boy. Ellie is feeding the baby."

Sandy blushed.

Miss Douglas blinked, shocked by Nick's directness. "It's her job to wait on us."

"Not today," Nick said.

Mrs. Douglas scowled.

Dr. Morgan smiled.

Inwardly, Ellie groaned as she stood. What would

Annie say if Nick chased away regular customers? "Mr. Baron, I don't mind cutting Sandy a piece of pie."

Nick shook his head. "He is a grown man very capable of doing for himself. The baby comes first."

She leaned closer to Nick and lowered her voice. "I've been serving folks since I was six. I can feed the baby and take care of everyone else."

Nick looked unrepentant. "Just because you can, doesn't mean you should," he said in a voice loud enough for everyone to hear.

Ellie's face turned crimson. *"It's my job."*

"Maybe you need a new one," Nick said.

The doctor laid his napkin by his plate. "Mr. Baron is right. You've got your hands full. I'd be happy to cut the pie for Sandy. Fact, I could use one myself."

"I'd like a piece, too, Dr. Morgan," said Miss Douglas.

Mrs. Douglas leaned over to her daughter and whispered something in her ear. Immediately the girl stood. "Why don't I help you?" she offered.

"My Robyn is an excellent cook," Mrs. Douglas purred.

"That so?" the doctor said, politely disinterested.

Miss Douglas set it on the table and stared down at it as if not sure what to do next.

The doctor handed her a knife. "This might be of help."

Miss Douglas took the knife. "Of course." She hacked out an uneven chunk of pie and handed it to her mother.

Her mother glanced down at the piece. She looked annoyed. "Thank you, dear."

Ellie cringed as she watched the girl chop through the pie that had taken her an hour to make.

Miss Douglas cut three more pieces and by the time she was finished, her fingernails were blue and her cuffs stained.

Sandy looked at his piece. "Looks like it was attacked by a bear." He took a bite. "But, as always, Miss Ellie's cooking is the best."

The doctor nodded. "The presentation is shaky but the taste is wonderful, Mrs. Watson."

Ellie blushed. "Thank you, Dr. Morgan."

"I only wish I could stop by more often," Dr. Morgan said.

Nick, who had filled a plate with stew, clanged the lid back down on the pot.

Mrs. Douglas's eyes narrowed as she sized up Ellie. "Mrs. Watson, wherever did you learn to cook so well?"

Ellie hesitated. "I guess I just picked it up over the years."

"Did your mother teach you?"

"Yes," Ellie lied.

"She must have been a wonderful woman," Mrs. Douglas said. The older woman seemed to sense that she'd touched a nerve. "Tell me about her."

Ellie wondered when the day would come when the lies would stop. "She was wonderful."

"And where'd you say you grew up? What's your maiden name?" Miss Douglas said. Her sweet voice belied the hardness in her eyes.

Nick cleared his throat. "Miss Douglas, how about a piece of pie? I could use one." His request sounded like a command.

The young girl hesitated as if she were waiting for Ellie's answer.

Nick locked his gaze on the young woman. She paled and, without argument, rose and cut him a piece of pie.

Ellie released the breath she'd been holding. She owed Nick.

"I shall be sure to make this stop a regular detour when I make my rounds," Dr. Morgan said cheerfully.

"You're always welcome," Ellie said.

"My daughter is looking forward to seeing more of you in town this winter, Dr. Morgan," Mrs. Douglas said.

"Yes," the doctor replied. "That would be lovely."

Mrs. Douglas didn't like the way the doctor's eyes lingered on Ellie. Her eyes narrowed to priggish slits. "I believe all this travel has robbed me of my appetite. We should go ahead and get back on the trail."

Miss Douglas looked up from the mutilated piece of pie she'd cut for herself. "But we've only just begun dessert."

Sandy looked up from his pie. He was clearly disappointed. "If you'll give me just a minute to enjoy this pie, then we can hit the road."

"I wish to go *now*," Mrs. Douglas said.

"I've changed your horses so you can leave immediately," Nick said. He might as well have told them to get off the property.

Ellie felt her stomach tumble. Annie had put her in charge of the stop and Nick was chasing away the first customers she'd been in charge of handling.

Mrs. Douglas, with her daughter in tow, started out of the cabin. Sandy and the doctor followed. Ellie was on their heels, the baby still in her arms.

Nick walked to the carriage. Ellie could have cheerfully killed him.

Sandy gobbled the last of his pie and set the plate on the front porch. "Thank you, Ellie. Sure do appreciate it." He eyed Nick. "Hope you catch up with that friend of yours *real* soon."

Dr. Morgan pulled on his hat. "I suppose you'll be leaving the valley soon, Mr. Baron." There was no mistaking his hopeful tone.

"Actually, I'm not. I've got a patch of land not ten miles from here. Once my business is settled, I plan to do a little ranching."

Ellie's jaw dropped. "You have land in the valley?"

He grinned. "I'm full of surprises."

Miss Douglas climbed into the carriage. Mrs. Douglas waited by the coach door, her hand extended for the doctor to take.

Dutifully, the doctor took her hand and helped her into the carriage. He turned to Ellie. "I look forward to seeing you soon."

"Thank you."

Ellie glanced toward the vehicle. The matter of the bill was always an awkward moment for Ellie. Annie had no trouble asking for money, but Ellie always felt sheepish about it. To make matters worse, the Douglases had used up their credit. Annie had warned them that going forward, they'd be cash only.

Ellie cleared her throat. "It'll be eight dollars, Mrs. Douglas."

"I shall give you my IOU," Mrs. Douglas said. "Do you have pen and paper?"

Ellie moistened her lips. She didn't like to argue,

but as Miss Adeline had said, business was business. "You told Annie you'd settle up on your return trip."

Mrs. Douglas raised a thick eyebrow as she peered through the coach window at Ellie. "Are you questioning my word? Everyone takes my credit."

"We can't extend any more credit."

Dr. Morgan reached into his pocket. "Let me pay my share. It's the least I can do."

The older woman lifted an eyebrow, summoning her iciest stare. "No, Dr. Morgan, I said I would settle your bill and I will. Mrs. Watson needs to understand that my husband will settle up when it's convenient."

"Take their packages off the top of the carriage, Sandy," Nick ordered. His tone left no room for argument.

"You will do no such thing!" Mrs. Douglas ordered.

Sandy's gaze flitted from the older woman to Nick. His face paled when he looked into Nick's eyes. "How many you want me to take down, Mr. Baron?"

"All of them."

"You will not!" Mrs. Douglas's face had turned red. "Mrs. Watson, this is an outrage."

"This is business," Nick said.

"You can have your bags back when you've paid your bill," Ellie said. Cash was too precious to pass up.

Mrs. Douglas glanced at the doctor and then pulled eight dollars out of her purse. She thrust them into Ellie's hand. "There. And we won't be stopping here again."

The doctor winked at Ellie and then climbed aboard. Mrs. Watson promptly closed the window curtain.

Ellie couldn't help but smile. Sandy put on his floppy hat and faced Ellie. He looked as if he wanted to say something, but with Nick standing so close, he appeared to lose his nerve. He touched the tip of his hat. "I will see you soon, Ellie. Next week, likely. Best of luck to you, Mr. Baron. I reckon we won't be crossing paths again."

Nick grinned. "Never is a long time."

Ellie ignored Nick and held out her hand to Sandy. He took it immediately. "It will be a pleasure."

He hesitated before he released her hand and climbed on top of his coach, took hold of the reins and released the brake. With one final wave, he drove off.

Nick watched the coach vanish on the horizon. "Both those men are sweet on you."

Ellie was surprised Nick had noticed or had bothered to comment. "Sandy has hinted that he'd like to court me. And the doctor kept talking about visiting more in the spring."

Nick grunted. "Neither would make you a good husband."

She arched an eyebrow, amazed at his gall. "How would you know? That is for me to judge."

His gaze lingered on hers an extra beat. "You need a man who knows and understands your past. A man who accepts you for exactly who you are. Dr. Morgan and Sandy would not accept your past."

Nick hit on a worry that had stalked her since she'd remade herself into a widow. She lifted her chin.

"You're already lying to them, *Mrs. Watson.*"

She sighed. She'd spun so many stories over the last couple of months, she'd started to lose track. But she had little choice. "The men who know about my past are never going to ask for my hand in marriage," she said, meeting his gaze.

"Don't bet on it."

Before she could respond, he walked back to the barn.

THAT NIGHT, Ellie sat on her bed cross-legged. Rose was asleep. Her bedroom door was closed. A lantern glowed on her side table.

She thought about what Nick had said today about Dr. Morgan and Sandy. He was right. Dr. Morgan was a kind man, but he was from the East and he wanted a respectable wife. Sandy was young, inexperienced and had put her up on a pedestal. If either knew she'd grown up in a brothel or that Rose's mother had been a whore, there was a good chance neither would accept her or Rose.

Perhaps she wasn't destined to marry. Perhaps it would always be just her and Rose.

Ellie picked up her brush from the side table and started to work the tangles from her hair. The bristles snagged in a knot. Her frustration grew. In her state of mind, she'd rip every knot out of her head. She tossed the brush into the drawer.

She was trapped between the past and the future.

She wanted to move forward and to make a new life, but her history wouldn't allow it.

Ellie noticed Jade's Bible in the drawer next to the brush. It was another reminder of her past. She picked it up. Carefully, she smoothed her hand over the gold cross embossed into the worn black leather. She'd had no time to look at the book since Jade had given it to her. And in truth, she'd been working so hard to forget her past that she'd wanted nothing to do with anything that linked her to it.

Once she'd nearly thrown away the Bible. It was proof that Rose wasn't hers by birth. But as tempted as she'd been, she'd hung on to it. Her own memories of her mother were vague at best and she'd have given anything to have something that had belonged to her. So she'd saved the Bible, unable to rob Rose of her only link to Jade.

Ellie opened the book and saw the date July 1, 1836, at the top. The lettering was thin and uneven, as if a very old person had written it. There were no words to explain the date.

She turned the pages, amazed at how thin they were. The book was well made and had likely cost a goodly sum.

She'd heard Bible stories read from time to time by traveling tent preachers and she knew the book was full of fantastic tales. One day she hoped to read them to Rose.

She closed the book and set it on the bed. That's when she noticed the tiniest slip of paper sticking out of the back. Curious, she flipped to the back of the book. To her surprise, the paper wasn't tucked between the last pages, but was hidden under the back binding of the book.

She laid the book down flat on the bed, leaned over it and studied the binding. Whoever had glued down the flap had done it quickly. She could see now that the top edge was also curling up.

Gently she peeled back the binding. Underneath it was the piece of paper. Unlike the Bible's yellowed pages, this paper was white and new. Clearly, it had been put in the book very recently.

Ellie unfolded it. At the top was a note written in a lovely script—a woman's handwriting. And below the text was a map. She studied the streets and realized she recognized the configuration. It was the town of Butte.

She scanned the text again, looking for any word that she might recognize. Then the letters G-O-L-D popped out at her. Gold!

Her heart started to hammer in her chest. Monty had said that Jade had hidden the gold.

Ellie closed her eyes, trying to remember Jade's last words. *Keep it safe and close to you. It's worth more than you can imagine.*

She studied the map again. By the looks of Jade's mark, the gold was hidden behind the livery off of Main Street. She pictured the location. There were piles of hay behind the livery, broken wagons and a shed. Jade's *X* showed exactly where it was hidden.

Ellie almost laughed.

She'd thought the book's value had been sentimental to Jade. Now she realized it was the key to the gold. Jade had wanted her daughter to have the money.

Ellie's head spun. This was the map Frank wanted. The one Nick wanted!

Excitement thrumming in her veins, she stood and moved toward her door. Her first reaction was to give the map to Nick. This map was the key to catching Frank. And the sooner Frank was caught, the sooner she'd have her reward money.

But as she reached for the door Rose whimpered in her sleep. Ellie stopped and checked on the baby. Gently she smoothed her fingertip over Rose's cheek. Her heart swelled. Lord, but there was so much she wanted to give this baby.

She straightened, clutching the map to her chest. If she gave this map to Nick, what assurance did she have that he'd give her the reward? His word? There was a powerful attraction between them, but that and ten cents would buy her a cup of coffee.

She sat on the bed, very carefully folded the map and tucked it into the back of the Bible. She put it in the chest under her bed.

The floorboards creaked as Nick's firm steps echoed in the house. She could hear him pause on the stairs and backtrack toward her room.

"You all right, Ellie?" he said.

Nick's deep voice sent a million prickles down her spine. Her gaze darted to the door. She half expected to see him standing there. He wasn't, but his shadow passed across the crack of light below the door.

"Everything's fine. Just settling in for the night."

He hesitated. "Good night to you then."

Her heart raced. "Good night."

She sat on her bed and pressed her palms to her burning cheeks. Lord, what was she thinking? Did she really want to be on the wrong side of someone like Nick Baron?

Ellie glanced down at the baby. She'd do whatever was needed to protect Rose's future.

Even cross Nick Baron.

CHAPTER TWELVE

THE NEXT MORNING Nick stood in front of the corral, filling the feed bin with fresh hay. Ever since the coach had left, he'd done little but think of Ellie. Her scent. The tone of her voice. The sound of her footsteps in the house. He found himself enjoying every detail about her.

There was a lot to admire about the woman. Yeah, she'd been a whore, but his past was far from perfect. She'd come to this valley to make a fresh start. And by his way of thinking, she was doing a mighty fine job.

Hadn't he come West for the same reason? To start over? Who was he to judge Ellie? He'd messed up his life good and fine before he'd come West. And he'd been born to money and privilege. Ellie had started with nothing and still she thrived.

Hell, if truth were told, Sandy and Dr. Morgan could very well forgive her her past. She was a woman any man would be lucky to have.

Until the doctor had talked of courting Ellie, Nick had not given any serious thought to marrying Ellie or any woman again. The doctor was a good man, but the idea that Ellie could belong to him or another man unsettled him. The realization that she wasn't his had him rethinking his distaste for marriage.

And truthfully, the more he thought about marrying Ellie, the more the idea appealed. She knew Montana. She was a fine mother. And her mind wasn't filled with fairy tales or dreams of knights in shining armor. From the start, she'd seen him at his worst and she'd stuck by him.

She'd said her price was marriage.

And he was willing to pay.

The question now was, would she have him?

Since he'd risen this morning, he'd been trying to muster the courage to talk to Ellie about the future. She'd talked of a café, but he wondered if she was fully committed to the idea.

Nick sighed. The sooner he talked to her, the sooner he'd have his answers. It wasn't like him to hesitate. When action needed to be taken, he took it. There'd been opportunities to speak to Ellie. And he'd let each one pass.

Ellie walked outside with a bucket of grain in her hand. As she headed toward the chicken coop, the wind teased the edge of her skirts and the ends of her hair, which she wore down and tied at the base of her neck.

His gut tightened. Like a lad in short pants, he nearly lost his nerve before frustration stoked his anger and pride. He dumped the last of the hay into the bin and strode toward her.

She was tossing cracked corn onto the ground for the chickens that pecked the dirt around her.

"Ellie."

She started. She didn't look up at him as she tossed more grain on the ground. "Yes?"

"There's something I want to talk to you about," he said.

Glancing up at him, he imagined he saw her stiffen for a moment. "What?"

"Frank Palmer."

She paled. "What about him?"

"It's not that I want to talk about him, but rather what you plan to do after I take him to jail."

She dropped her gaze to the pail and dug out another handful of grain. Absently she let the grain slip from her fingers. "Like I said, I thought of opening that café in town."

He shoved his hands into his pockets. The words that needed saying were on the tip of his tongue, but he couldn't seem to speak them. If Bobby were alive, the old coot would have been laughing until he was sick.

"I've got property not far from here. I've not seen the land, but there is supposed to be a cabin there. It's near a stream. Lots of grassland."

"It sounds lovely." Ellie started to walk toward the coop. He followed.

She tossed another handful of grain to the chickens. "So what do you plan to do on this bit of land that you own?"

"Raise horses."

Nervous, she tucked a curl behind her ear. "You have a way with them."

"I grew up around them."

"Ah." She was tense.

And he felt like a schoolboy. "When I start working this land, it's going to be a new beginning for me."

"I'm glad for you."

"It could be a fresh start for you, as well."

She frowned. "I don't understand."

"You and Rose could come with me. We could marry. Be a family."

Ellie took a step back. Clearly this was the last thing she'd expected him to say. "You said you'd never marry again."

"Things change."

She frowned. "Nick, you don't know me. Why the devil would you propose marriage?"

"I know you better than just about anyone."

She frowned. "No, you don't."

"If there were ever two people who've seen the worst of each other, it's us."

She looked as if she wanted to say something, then stopped herself. "For as long as I live, there will be men who recognize me from the Silver Slipper."

"You're honest and hardworking. You love that baby. There's not much more a man wants from a wife."

"You make me sound like I'm something special. I'm not."

"I know where I stand with you, Ellie. You know the worst of my past and you've accepted it. I can't say that about anyone else."

"I'm not so perfect, Nick."

"Exactly. Neither am I. And I suspect we'll have our share of fights. But we are suited to each other."

She sighed. "I don't know."

He tugged her closer to him until her chest touched his. Gently he tipped her head back until her lips were only inches from his.

He lowered his lips to hers, savoring her softness and sweet taste.

She didn't pull away. Encouraged, he coaxed open her lips with his tongue and deepened the kiss.

A soft sound rumbled in her chest as she leaned into him. The basket dropped to the ground when he banded his arm around her shoulders and pulled her tight against him. She wrapped her arms around his neck and rose up on her tiptoes.

He cupped her breast and rubbed his thumb over her nipple. Even through the calico he could feel it harden and pucker.

Ellie's passion matched his own.

He picked her up and, still kissing her, carried her into the house. His eyes adjusted quickly to the dim light as he moved toward her room. He laid her in the center of the bed. She stared up at him. Her eyes were filled with desire.

He reached for the hem of her skirt and pulled it up. His erection throbbed against her threadbare pantaloons.

He'd wanted this—her—since the moment he'd seen her outside the Silver Slipper. "On the trail I dreamed of doing this to you," he said, his voice a ragged whisper.

She stared up at him with half-hooded eyes. She moistened her lips. Without saying a word, she lifted her hips and pressed them against his.

He reached inside the waistband of her pantaloons and pressed his fingers against her center. Her velvet folds were moist. He thought he'd explode with desire.

"I shouldn't do this." She reached for the buckle

of his pants and unfastened it. Her small hand slid inside his pants and rubbed his hardness.

He was ready to be rid of his clothes. "You're the one person I would never hurt. I trust you with my life."

She stiffened. "Don't say that, please."

Nick searched her face, confused by the tension in her voice. "What is it?"

Ellie pressed her palms against his chest. "Stop."

"Why?" Every muscle in his body snapped with desire.

"I just can't do this."

He stroked her hair. "I will make it good between us. You don't have to be afraid."

She closed her eyes. "No, I can't."

Somehow he found the strength to roll away from her. She scurried off the bed.

Before he could question her, Rose's piercing cry sliced through the house.

Ellie quickly righted her skirts, ran to her room and scooped Rose up from the cradle at the foot of the bed. The child continued to cry.

Nick shook off the desire, wishing like hell he understood women better. He followed her as he refastened his belt buckle. "Is she all right?"

"She feels warm."

Nick laid his hand on the baby's head. It was

warm and her cheeks were flushed. "What do you think it is?"

The desire had vanished from Ellie's eyes. Fear had taken its place. "I don't know. She was fine when I put her down."

Her eyes looked a little wild, as if she'd reached the end of her tether. She moved out into the great room, jostling the baby as she walked.

Nick washed his hands and made the bottle. It took him a few minutes longer than Ellie, but he managed the task. An odd sense of satisfaction curled in his gut as he handed the bottle to her.

Ellie tried to coax the nipple into Rose's mouth. The baby suckled twice and then she started to wail louder.

Ellie set the bottle aside and touched her lips to the baby's forehead. "I think she is getting warmer."

Nick crouched by the rocker. He laid his hand on the child's head. It was indeed warm. "Let me have a look in her mouth."

"Why?"

"Trust me."

She hesitated before she raised Rose's head so that he could smooth his finger along the baby's tiny gums. He felt two distinct ridges on the gumline. And as he rubbed the ridges, the baby's cries eased. "She's cutting teeth."

"Teeth? Why would teeth make her so miserable?"

He cupped the child's head. So tiny. "I don't know. I remember when my sister's teeth came in. Julia had a time with hers. She cried like her mouth was on fire each time she grew a tooth."

His heart tightened when he thought of Julia. He often wondered what had become of her over the years.

"But Rose is so young," Ellie said.

"Babies can get teeth this early."

"So what do we do?"

"Not much we can do. Keep trying to give her the bottle. The teeth should break through soon and when they do, she should be fine."

She looked at him, gratitude in her eyes. "Thank you. I don't know what I would have done if you hadn't been here."

His heart swelled with pride. "We make a good team."

She held his gaze. "Nick, I don't know."

"I'm not asking for your answer now. When Frank's in jail, we'll talk again."

FRANK RODE into the small mining town at a quarter past noon. Saddle sore and hungry, he wanted nothing more than to have a hot meal and put up his feet for a spell.

But he didn't have time for either. He was close to finding his Ellie, the baby and the gold—he could feel it in his bones. His life was finally coming together.

Frank rode to the mercantile and dismounted. He tied the reins of his horse to the post and went inside. The store smelled of coffee, spices and cured ham. His stomach rumbled.

There was no one behind the long counter lined with jars. He strode toward it, opened a jar and popped a peppermint into his mouth.

"That'll be a penny."

The high-handed voice came from his right. A tall, thin man stepped into the shop from a side door. He wore a white shirt and black pants, and his thinning black hair was greased to his head. He carried a sack of flour.

The man's tone goaded his temper. Uppity folks never sat well with him. Frank took another piece of candy.

"That'll be two cents."

"I'm looking for a woman. She's got real red hair and can cook real well."

"No one in town like that." The shopkeeper moved the jar under the counter.

Frank could feel his patience thinning. He wanted to be done with this business and he wanted his gold now. "You sure about that?"

Frowning, the storekeeper thrummed his fingers on the counter. "I don't know anyone like that. Women are as rare as hen's teeth out here and if there was a redheaded cook in town, I'd know it."

Frank shoved aside his disappointment. He'd been to a dozen other towns like this one and he'd had no luck finding Ellie. Still, he wasn't going to give up. "Appreciate the information." He turned to leave.

"Hey, are you going to pay for that, *mister?*"

The shopkeeper's tone set his blood on fire. He faced the man, his hand sliding to his gun. Then he caught himself. He'd promised himself that he'd turn over a new leaf now that he was going to be a family man. No more violence.

Frank dug in his pocket, pulled out two pennies and laid them on the counter. "There you go."

He started toward the door, proud that he'd not lost his temper. Yes, sir, he was going to be a fine husband and father.

The storekeeper jingled the pennies in his hand. "That all you gonna buy?"

Frank managed a smile. He reckoned the Almighty Himself was testing his temper. "Won't be needing anything else."

The shopkeeper snorted. "Men like you are more trouble than you are worth."

Frank's temper flared. *Leave. Just keep walking.*

Just keep walking. He twisted the knob. "Best of luck."

"Don't come back here!"

Frank snapped. In one fluid motion he drew his gun with one hand as he crossed the room. He reached across the counter and grabbed the store-keeper by the collar with the other. He pressed the gun to the keeper's cheek. The clerk dropped the pennies. They pinged against the floor.

"I don't appreciate your tone, mister. I'm doing my best to be kind toward you, but you ain't being very respectful. I am a paying customer and I deserve respect." He put his face right up to the man's. "Where I come from, we gut fish like you."

The storekeeper choked and sputtered. His eyes looked as if they'd pop out of his head. "Sorry."

Frank shook his head. "Sorry? You insult me and all you can say is sorry? What good does *sorry* do me?"

"Take the candy," the clerk said. "It's on the house."

Frank loosened his hold. "Now that's more like it."

The man rubbed his neck, which was red with Frank's fingerprints. He returned the jar to the counter. "Take all the candy you want, mister, but just leave."

Frank started to fill his pockets with candy. "You sure you don't know nothing about a redheaded woman in these parts?"

The shopkeeper's Adam's apple bobbed in his throat when he swallowed. "Head toward Thunder Canyon. There's a coach stop there that's run by a woman named Annie. She'd know about your redhead if she were within a hundred miles of here."

Frank scooped up another handful of candy and shoved it into his pocket. "Where's this stop?"

"About two days due west."

"Appreciate the help." He holstered his gun.

The storekeeper glanced at the candy jar and then at Frank's grimy hands. Whatever he wanted to say, he swallowed.

"While I'm at it, why don't you wrap me up a couple of cans of beans, ham and biscuits?"

The storekeeper moved to the end of the counter and chose four cans of beans. He placed them in a sack along with the other provisions.

Laughing, Frank scooped up the sack. "Put it on my account."

The shopkeeper's gaze traveled the length of Frank's body. "W-what do you w-want with this woman?" he stammered.

"She's my wife."

CHAPTER THIRTEEN

LATER THAT DAY, Ellie sat back on her heels and stared at the even rows of vegetables, wiping beads of sweat from her forehead. Her old work dress had dried and she'd changed into it. It hung on her like a sack and made her feel ugly.

She had enough work to keep three people busy, yet concentrating on a task as simple as pulling weeds was nearly impossible.

Nick's marriage proposal kept ringing in her head. *Marriage.*

Lord, it was the last thing she'd ever expected from him.

His offer should have made her happy. It's what she'd wanted only yesterday. However, his proposal fed the festering guilt she'd harbored since she'd found the gold map.

Ellie glanced toward the corral, where Nick was shoeing the black mare. He was good with the horses. He possessed patience and a firmness that they responded to. Even Onyx had fallen under Nick's spell. She obeyed his every command and seemed almost eager to please.

Ellie wondered if she had fallen under a spell, as well. Several times today she'd nearly tossed good sense aside and told him about the map.

Yet each time she went to get it, she stopped herself. Growing up without a family had taught her to look after herself. Loneliness and fear of the future had trained her to play her cards carefully because once they were on the table, there was no taking them back.

Keeping the map was the smart thing to do. She wanted to believe Nick's offer was genuine, but what if he were playing her just to get the gold?

So why did she feel so bad? And so lost? So cheap, as if she'd sold her soul?

The sound of horses in the distance had her rising. Shielding her eyes with her hand, she saw that two riders approached.

Nick came out of the corral. He'd heard the riders, too. He moved toward her, his hand resting on his gun.

Ellie's heart jumped as he stood beside her. Power radiated from his body. She felt safe beside him.

"More people pass through here than a New York City train station. Any guesses as to who it is this time?" he asked.

The plume of dust clouded around the riders, making it difficult to see who it was. "No."

"I will never get used to strangers coming and going here," Nick said.

The riders moved closer. Ellie squinted. "It's Annie and Mike!" A wave of relief washed over her. She'd never been happier to see anyone in her life.

Nick's lips flattened into a grim line. "I thought they weren't supposed to return for a couple more weeks."

"I did, too. I hope everything went well."

Within minutes Annie and Mike arrived in the front yard. Annie's gaze swept over Nick. She frowned, clearly not happy at the sight of an unexpected stranger. Mike's hand slid to the gun at his side. His body was rigid.

Ellie ran up to Annie. "My heavens! It's so good to see you! Is everything all right with your parents?"

Annie hugged Ellie with a mother's protectiveness. "They're fine. I'm more concerned about what's going on here. Are you all right?"

"I am now." Ellie's voice tightened with emotion. Somewhere along the way Annie had silently stepped into the role of Ellie's mother. Ellie had not realized until this moment how much she needed a mother's love.

Annie gave her an extra squeeze and then stepped back. "Who's he?"

Ellie wiped a tear from her eyes. "This is Nick Baron."

Nick stepped forward. "You must be Annie," he said formally.

Annie's gaze narrowed. "I've heard the name before."

"So have I," Mike said. He tightened his hold on the handle of his pistol. "He's the bounty hunter."

Nick nodded. "I've a reputation."

"A mighty bad one," Mike said. "What are you doing here?"

Ellie blinked back the tears in her eyes. "Mr. Baron has been here for over a week. When he arrived, he kinda caught me by surprise and I shot him."

Annie's eyes shone with respect for Ellie.

"Looking back, I'd say I deserved it," Nick answered.

"It was a misunderstanding," Ellie added.

"I want to hear all about," Mike said. His gaze bore into Nick.

"Let's get settled in," Annie said, sensing Mike's anger.

"I'll unsaddle the horses," Mike said. "How about a hand, *Nick?*"

Nick didn't argue. "Sure."

Annie pulled off her leather gloves. "Ellie and I will check on the baby."

The men went to the barn and the women inside. Ellie checked on the baby, who lay asleep in her cradle, then joined Annie in the kitchen. "I can feel your worry over here."

Annie set her saddlebag on the table. "Nick Baron is the last man I expected to see at the cabin. Do you have any idea who he is?"

"A bounty hunter."

"Not just *any* bounty hunter, Ellie. He's got one of the fiercest reputations in Montana."

"So I'm learning."

"The Indians call him the Ghost Tracker because he moves as silent as a spirit."

"I've learned that lesson firsthand a couple of times."

Annie fiddled with the cuff of her dress. "How'd he end up here?"

"It's a long story."

"I'm not going anywhere." She sat at the table and made herself comfortable.

Ellie's stomach ached at the thought of explaining her past. But Nick was linked to her past and it was time Annie learned the truth. "I'm not a widow, as I've claimed to be."

Annie was silent.

"I came from Butte, not Helena." She hesitated, wishing with all her heart she didn't have to tell the rest. No matter how hard she tried, the Silver Slipper kept creeping back into her life. "I grew up in a brothel called the Silver Slipper."

"I've heard of it."

"My mother worked there. She died when I was six. The madam, Miss Adeline, put me to work in the kitchens." She hesitated, half expecting a look of shock and horror on Annie's face. She saw none.

"About two months ago," Ellie continued, "Miss Adeline asked me to attend a woman named Jade, who was very pregnant and in labor. Jade had once been a whore at the Silver Slipper and had left when an outlaw named Monty Palmer married her."

Ellie felt as if she were describing a dream. Jade seemed to be far away. "The labor went well, but she started bleeding badly. She knew she was dying and she asked me to take her baby."

"Rose," Annie said.

"Yes."

"I was scared out of my wits, but I gave her my word. I was headed down the back staircase with Rose when Monty's brother, Frank, came into the brothel looking for Monty and Jade. Frank demanded his gold from Monty and when he realized his brother didn't know anything about it, he shot him in the heart. I didn't stick around to find out what happened next. I started running and I ended up here."

"How does Nick Baron figure into this?"

"The gold was stolen from the railroad. A good friend of Nick's was killed during the robbery." And she had the map. Ellie felt awful.

"And he figured out you were the last to see Jade alive and he tracked you here?"

"Yes." Ellie smoothed her damp palms over her hips. "I'm sorry I lied to you, but I was so desperate for a place to stay. I know how it is when people find out you've lived at the Silver Slipper. I never worked the upstairs rooms, but anyone with a connection to that place is branded a whore." Tears welled in Ellie's eyes and spilled down her face.

Annie stood and wrapped her arms around Ellie. "I knew there was more to your story than you let on. But I could see you had a good heart. I could see you loved your daughter."

"I wanted to tell you so many times."

"You were protecting Rose. I would have done the same for my own daughter."

Ellie hugged Annie tight.

Tears glistened in Annie's blue eyes when she pulled back. "So now you and Mr. Baron are waiting for this Frank?"

"Yes."

"I do not like this. It is very dangerous for you."

"Nick has said he will protect us."

Annie met her gaze. "What else is there between you and this Mr. Baron?"

Ellie blushed. "He has asked me to marry him."

Annie arched an eyebrow, careful not to offer an opinion.

"I said no."

The older woman shook her head. "He is not the kind of man who accepts no."

"He says he will ask me again after Frank has been caught."

"I thought so."

"In truth, he makes me feel things I've never felt before. He says he wants to set his gun aside and start a ranch near here."

Annie shook her head.

"I know, I know. I've seen men make promises and break them. He even promised to give me the reward money. It is one thousand dollars. I want to give you half."

Annie shrugged. "I have my coach stop and now I have Mike. I need no more."

Ellie sniffed. "Here I am going on about myself and I've not asked you about your father. Is he all right?"

"He will live to be one hundred. He refuses to slow down, which only drives my mother crazy." Annie grinned. "I think sometimes he enjoys making Mother angry so that he can see the fire in her eyes."

"And what of you and Mike?" Ellie prompted.

Annie blushed. "He has asked me to marry him."

"And you said yes."

"We celebrated our union in an Arapaho ceremony so that my parents could be present. The ceremony was enough for me, but Mike wants a preacher to say his sacred words and bless our union, as well. That is why we came back. I wanted you to be present."

Ellie was touched. "Me?"

"You and Rose are my family, too. The daughter and granddaughter of my heart."

Ellie's throat tightened.

"I don't know if you know, but I gave birth to a daughter long ago." Annie's voice was whisper-soft. "My baby's father was my first husband and he owned this coach stop. He was much older than me, but he was so brave and strong. Indians and whites alike respected him. I loved him very much." Emotion forced her to pause. "When our little girl became sick and died, it broke Nathan's heart. He could no longer look at me without great sadness. He stopped sharing my bed and started drinking heavily." Tears welled in her eyes. "I could not bear his grief and mine, so I packed up my belongings and went home to my mother. I'd dreamed my husband would follow, that we would put our grief aside and we'd make more children. But he never came after me. Three months after I left, word reached me he had been killed trying to save a child drowning in the river."

"Oh, Annie, I am so sorry."

"I returned to Spring Rock and kept the stop going as a tribute to him. For many years I mourned both my daughter and my husband. Then I met Mike and my heart opened up."

Ellie hugged her again. "This is wonderful!"

Her gaze was bittersweet. "The wedding will be a simple affair. We passed a stage a day's ride back. A preacher rode beside the stage on his horse. He has agreed to stop here and perform the ceremony."

Ellie's heart swelled. "I will make you a special cake to celebrate the day."

"You don't have to go to any trouble."

"But I must! You are like a mother to me and I cannot let your wedding go uncelebrated."

The brightness in Annie's eyes made her look years younger. "I do love him."

"I know." She grinned. "I've known since the first day I saw you look at him."

Her hands went to her cheek. "Was I that obvious?"

"To me, yes."

Annie laughed. She reached inside her saddlebag and pulled out a beaded pouch. The leather was faded and the beads had lost some of their luster, but Ellie could see that the workmanship was very fine. "I want to give you something."

"You've already given me so much. I can't accept anything else."

"You will if you wish to make me happy." Annie loosened the ties on the pouch. She removed a gold nugget that was shaped like an eagle. She placed the nugget in Ellie's hand.

"This gold must be worth a fortune."

"I suppose it is," she said. "I haven't really worried about its monetary value."

"I can't accept this." Ellie held out the nugget to Annie.

Annie made no move to accept it. "Years ago, my mother gave this to me as a wedding gift. I was deeply honored by it. I believed the gold was the source of my happiness and I guarded it closely. I began to fear that I would lose my perfect life if I lost the nugget. I guarded it jealously and refused to pass it on when there were others who could have benefited from its magic." She sighed. "When I lost my daughter and husband, my grief was so great, I began to believe the nugget had cursed me for my selfishness. The night before I returned to Spring Rock, I tossed it into the woods."

The gold nugget felt smooth and warm to Ellie's fingers.

"My mother found it and saved it," Annie said. "She knew one day I would come home and claim it." She smiled. "An hour after she gave it to me, Mike proposed. Now, I want you to have it."

Ellie was deeply touched. "I can't accept this."

"You are a kind, honorable woman, and if my daughter had lived, I could only hope she would be as brave and honest as you are."

Ellie glanced at the golden rock. Tears streamed down her face. "I'm not a good person."

Annie hugged her. "Of course you are."

She pulled out of Annie's embrace and replaced the nugget in its pouch. "There is something I must tell you. I have one last secret to share."

Annie said nothing.

Ellie retrieved Jade's Bible from her room and returned to Annie. "This is the book Rose's mother gave me."

Annie watched as Ellie opened the book to the back and then peeled away the binding. Ellie removed the map and laid it on the table next to the book.

"What is this?" Annie said.

Carefully, Ellie unfolded it and smoothed it flat. "It is a map that Jade drew. It shows the place where she hid the gold. Nick tells me the gold is worth nearly twenty thousand dollars."

"You have not told Nick about this."

"No."

"Why not?"

"When he arrived, I knew nothing about the map. I only found it last night."

Annie frowned. "And you have not given it to him because you do not trust him."

"I want to so much, but trust is so hard for me. I've spent my life in a brothel. I have seen only the worst of men."

"You are afraid. This I understand. It is natural to think you'd never have to worry about money again."

"I could give Rose so much."

Annie shrugged. "You have already given her everything she needs." She laid her hands on Ellie's shoulders and looked directly into her eyes. "If you keep this gold, it will poison your heart. And then you will not be the kind of mother Rose deserves."

Ellie already felt tainted by the gold.

"Even if you find the gold," Annie continued, "you would spend your life worrying that someone else would steal it. You would treat this treasure like I treated the gold nugget. It will not bring you happiness."

The baby started to fuss. "Let me get her," Annie said. "I have missed my Rose." Annie went to Ellie's room and came out with the child on her shoulder. The baby quieted. "I think you must go find Nick and have a talk with him."

Annie was right. The gold wasn't hers to keep. It never had been and she'd been a fool to think it ever could be hers.

She stared at the worn map, wondering what Nick would say when she told him she'd kept this secret.

At that moment she felt the hairs on the back of her neck rise. Her heart jumped and she turned.

Nick stood behind her. Ghost Tracker. He'd moved into the cabin so silently she'd not heard him.

His gaze flickered from her flushed cheeks to the paper in her hands. He took the map from her hand and studied it. His lips flattened into a grim line. "And to think I actually believed you were an innocent in all this."

The anger and disappointment in his face sliced at her heart. "I didn't realize I had it until last night. Jade had hidden it in the back of the Bible she gave me."

He shook his head and grabbed the map. "Save your story for someone who cares. Right now, I've had my fill of lying whores."

CHAPTER FOURTEEN

ELLIE HAD BEEN CALLED a *whore* many times before, but the word had never cut her to the bone as it did now. She stood rigid, her limbs locked. She felt as if she could shatter into a million pieces.

From the threshold, she watched Nick hurry toward the barn. His broad shoulders were stiff. The map was clenched in his left fist.

"I should shoot him for speaking to you like that," Annie said. Rose was on her shoulder, trying to lift her small head.

"He's angry."

"That gives him no right."

Ellie shook her head. "I owe Nick an explanation." The disappointment and pain in his eyes would be seared in her memory forever.

Hearing the sadness in Ellie's voice, Annie sighed. "Then go after him," Annie said. "You will have no peace until you talk to him."

"I don't know what to say to him."

"If you care about him, you will find the right words."

If she cared about him. She did care about him. Her feelings for Nick were strong and powerful.

She closed her eyes. Nick Baron was dark and dangerous. And yes, honorable, with a code he would never break. God help her, but she didn't want to lose him.

"Do you love him?" Annie said.

Ellie's eyes snapped open. "No! He is the worst possible man for me to love. Nick flirts with danger so casually. I always dreamed of someone stable and kind, like Dr. Morgan."

Annie sighed as she patted Rose on the back. "One way or another, you must resolve things with Nick."

"I was so worried about him lying to me. And in the end I lied to him. He's so angry."

"If he is worthy of you, he will see past his anger and find forgiveness in his heart," Annie said.

Tears cascaded down Ellie's cheeks. "I don't know if he can forgive me. No one has ever looked at me with such hate before."

"He feels betrayed."

An overwhelming sense of loneliness choked the breath from her. "What if he doesn't forgive me?"

Annie, with Rose lying against her shoulder,

stood beside her. "Between men and women, there can only be great anger when there is great love. He would not have gotten so angry if his feelings for you didn't run deep." Annie set her jaw. "However, I would dearly love to give him a good thrashing for causing you such distress."

A smile tipped the edges of Ellie's lips. She pictured her petite friend thrashing Nick Baron. "For his own protection, I better go talk to him."

NICK SWORE as he stood by the corral. He stared off at the horizon. His blood boiled and he could feel a vein pulsing in his neck.

Ellie had lied to him!

Like Crystal and Gregory before him, she'd betrayed him!

He should have seen this coming a mile off, but he hadn't. From the moment he'd met her, he'd been off balance. His guard had been lowered. God help him, but he'd felt a connection to her.

His feelings had blinded him to the possibility that she was lying. Since he'd come to Montana, he'd been so careful not to trust anyone. There'd been no sloppy mistakes with any woman.

Footsteps sounded behind him. He didn't have to know who stood there. It was Ellie. Somewhere along the way her scent, her presence, had become so familiar to him. It was as if they'd known each other a lifetime.

"Miss Adeline always said when a man's angry it's best to leave him be and let him cool off."

His jaw tightened and released. "Maybe you best listen to that advice."

Ellie moved beside him. She leaned against the fence, staring in the same direction he did. He could feel her warmth and, despite his anger, he grew hard just thinking about touching her. "I've never been good at taking advice. Miss Adeline always said I was hardheaded and single-minded."

He wasn't going to soften toward her. "Where is this going, Ellie?"

"I came here to apologize."

"Why should you? You were doing exactly what I should have expected you to do. You were looking out for yourself."

"You're right, I was."

A thick silence fell between them and for several minutes Nick did his best to nurture his anger. "I was honest with you from the first."

"Except for the little white lie about you being a marshal."

He set his jaw. "It's not the same."

"Isn't it? You felt desperate. And I've felt a little

desperate these last months." Her voice was quiet, as if the admission had cost her.

Nick kept his gaze nailed to the horizon for fear that if he looked at her, he would melt. "How long have you known about the map?"

"Not even a full twenty-four hours. I found it last night at bedtime."

Damn his hide, but he wanted to believe her.

"I didn't know the map was in the Bible when Jade gave it to me. She told me it belonged to her grandmother—that it was a family heirloom."

Nick snorted. "Jade grew up in an orphanage in New York. She never knew her family."

Ellie blinked, shocked by the information. "She sounded so genuine. I really thought she meant everything she said." She frowned. "She told me Rose was the best thing that ever happened to her."

Nick swallowed. "Likely, that part was true. Jade was a cold, calculating woman who never gave anything to anyone. She wouldn't have given you the map if she hadn't trusted you and wanted the best for Rose."

"Then why not tell me about the map?"

"Jade always worked the angles. Maybe she figured Frank was on your heels. If you didn't know where the gold was, then you couldn't tell him. Jade hated Frank with a vengeance."

Ellie nodded. "Jade used to make fun of him when he visited the brothel. She hated the way he would just sit and stare at the girls. It bothered her that he never bought time with any of them."

This was new information to Nick. "He never spent time with the women?"

"No."

"What would he do?"

"He always ordered a big meal, but he wouldn't sit in the dining room with the other customers. He'd sit silent in the kitchen and eat while I worked."

Ellie's information fit with what he knew. "Frank and Monty's parents lost their farm back in '63. Frank always wanted to return to Missouri a rich man. The gold was his ticket back."

"Honestly, I wish I'd never heard of the gold."

"Why didn't you tell me this information about Frank before?"

"I didn't think it mattered much that he liked his steak rare and his potatoes with extra salt."

Nick rubbed the back of his neck. He looked down at her. The sunlight caught her red curls, making them look so vibrant. The freckles over the bridge of her nose combined with her pale, smooth skin had a devastating effect on him.

This softness he had for her angered him. Never

before had he felt so vulnerable. Not even with Crystal. How could he ever believe her again?

"I'm not sure what you expect from me." His voice held a bite he'd not expected.

She lifted her chin. Pride radiated from her. "I don't expect anything from you. I came to give you my apologies, is all. I should have given you the map right off." She turned to leave.

Before he thought, he reached out and took her arm in his. She stopped and looked up at him. The emotion in her eyes was as clear as the words on a page. Hope. Sorrow. Longing.

Unable to resist, he pulled her to him. She stood so close, the tips of her breasts brushed his chest. The top of her head barely reached his shoulders. He pushed her chin up so that he could see her lips. So smooth and round.

He leaned his face forward and gently kissed her. He wanted nothing more than to lose himself in her.

Nick savagely reined in his emotions. She was his Achilles' heel. He broke the kiss and stepped back.

She looked confused and disappointed. "Why did you stop?"

He stabbed his fingers through his hair. "I can't seem to control myself when I'm with you."

Her lips glistened with the moisture from their kiss. "Is that so bad?"

"Yes."

His raw honesty had her looking deeper into his eyes.

He swallowed, sure he could drown in those eyes. "God help me, but I've been through all this with my wife Crystal. Hell, it could have been July, she could have told me it was snowing, and I'd have believed her."

She didn't speak.

"Her lies and deceptions nearly killed me. I won't go through that again."

"All I can do is say I'm sorry. Lying is not my way."

"Then why lie to me? Why didn't you trust *me?*"

She met his gaze head-on. "Because you scare the living daylights out of me. I've been surrounded by men all my life. I've had more marriage proposals than I could count, but I've never had anyone throw me off balance like you have. For the first time, I understand how a woman can lose herself to a man. And I swore I'd never do that."

"You do the same to me and I don't like it one bit."

She took a step back. "Maybe we're too damaged to love or trust anyone."

The truth wasn't pretty. "Maybe."

"Maybe it's best things didn't work out between us."

He frowned. "Maybe."

Her breath hitched in her throat and for a moment she didn't speak. Finally she said, "I'll keep my distance from you until this mess with Frank is resolved. After that, I wish you the best."

He watched her walk back to the cabin with her back straight. So proud and tall.

Nick swallowed a lump in his throat and stared at the horizon again. Jagged mountains scraped the vivid blue sky. The sight of Ellie walking away was more painful than he could have ever imagined.

He crushed the gold map in his hand. He could put out enough information in the right places and soon Frank would know he had the gold, not Ellie. Frank's greed would flush him out. And then Nick would capture him.

His business would be done.

He could get on with his life.

And he'd never see Ellie again.

The plan was perfect. And he knew in his heart it would work.

So why did he feel like hell?

ELLIE COULDN'T SLEEP that night. Everyone was asleep—Nick in his spare room, Mike in another and Annie in her room.

Tomorrow the minister would arrive. Annie and Mike would be married. Nick would leave.

She rolled onto her side and punched her pillow. Why should she care if Nick Baron walked out of her life or not? Sure she cared about him, but it wasn't as if she loved the man.

Love.

The word flashed in her head like a streak of lightning.

Love.

Annie had asked her if she loved Nick. No, she did not love Nick Baron. Women who fell in love with men like him were foolish and, if anything, she was smart in the ways of men. Yes, she might have a weak spot for him, but love?

Unable to sleep, she sat up and lit a lantern. She glanced in the cradle at Rose. Satisfied the baby slept, she pulled on her robe. She'd expected to rise early in the morning to make Annie and Mike's cake. She should grab what sleep she could now.

But she knew herself well enough to know that she'd not sleep tonight. Her mind and body were far too restless.

She moved quietly into the kitchen, careful not to wake anyone. She pulled out the mixing bowls. She collected the butter she'd churned just days ago, flour, the precious little sugar she had, along with the baking soda and salt. Luckily the chickens had produced well this week and there were enough eggs. Normally, she'd have had to hoard them for days.

She measured the butter and sugar into a large wooden bowl and started to cream them with a spoon.

Ellie heard footsteps. She paused, torn between worry that it was Nick and guilt that she'd woken Mike or Annie.

Annie padded into the kitchen, pulling on a robe as she moved. "Can't sleep?"

Ellie set the bowl on the table. "I'd hoped I wouldn't wake you."

Annie shook her head. "No, I wasn't asleep anyway. These last two weeks, I've gotten used to having Mike by my side. I miss him."

"Why isn't he with you tonight?"

"He wanted to wait until the preacher said his sacred words over our union."

"Have you and Mike thought about what you'll do after the wedding tomorrow? I know he has a place in town."

"The town has too many people for me. And since he can keep his coach and horses here, there's no reason why he can't live at the coach stop."

"That makes sense."

Soon Mike would want Annie alone in their new home, without Ellie and Rose underfoot. He would never ask them to leave, but he would long for privacy with his wife.

Ellie and Rose would have to leave. She had suspected for weeks now that this time would come, but now that it was here, she felt great sadness. The coach stop had been her first real home.

In a second bowl, she measured out two cups of flour. Her movements were slow and deliberate. Concentrating on the cake was easier than thinking about her and Rose's future.

"I can see your mind working," Annie said. "You have nothing to worry about. There will always be a place for you here at the coach stop."

Annie's kindness touched her. She knew Annie meant everything she said. "A newly married couple deserves their own home."

Annie shook her head. "Mike and I have already talked about this. He wants you and Rose to stay. We've talked about building another room onto the house."

Ellie cracked two eggs into the batter. "Annie, that is so kind of you. But it's not right."

"Nonsense. I won't hear another word from you. You and Rose are staying."

Ellie smiled, but she was already thinking ahead. "Your life is moving on and I am so glad. But Rose and I don't belong here."

Annie looked stricken. "You are like my daughter, my family. It would break my heart to see you leave."

A tear fell down Ellie's cheek. "Daughters leave home. You left your mother's home."

Tears glistened in Annie's eyes. "But I only just found you."

"I am not going far away," she said, swallowing the new tears burning her throat.

"I don't want you to go."

"We will go into town. I'll open a café with my reward money. We will be fine. I promise."

Annie sniffed and shook her head. "My mother always said that one day I would understand how she felt when I left home. Now I do."

Ellie laid her hand on Annie's arm, which felt cold. "And one day Rose will leave me and I know I will come here and cry on your shoulder. It is the way of the world."

The women hugged.

Ellie pulled back. "Now stop, you are going to make me cry and I have a cake to bake."

"What can I do to help? I have never been much of a baker, but I want to help."

Ellie smiled, grateful that they would share this simple task. "Stoke the fires in the stove and bring me that tin of cinnamon."

The women worked side by side for the next hour. Neither spoke of Ellie's impending move, but the changes that would soon come to their lives weighed heavily on their minds.

Annie finally retired just after midnight, but Ellie stayed up until the cakes baked to a golden brown. She set them on the kitchen table and, as they cooled, she mixed the brown sugar icing. When she'd finished, she couldn't help but admire her work. The cake was one of the best she'd ever made and pride welled inside her.

Rose woke and Ellie mixed a bottle and fed the girl. She held her close, savoring the soft scent of milk and the sound of the baby suckling.

When Ellie finished feeding the baby, she crawled into bed just after two in the morning. The cabin smelled of warm cinnamon. Her muscles ached but her mind spun.

Nick had become such a part of her life in such a short time. And soon he'd be gone.

What would she do without him?

NICK KNEW the instant Ellie shut off her lantern downstairs. Wide awake, he lay in his bed, his hands tucked behind his head. For the past couple of hours he'd stared at the shadows slashing across the ceiling while he'd listened to Ellie move around the kitchen.

He'd also heard everything she'd said to Annie.

Sighing, he rolled on his side. He closed his eyes but knew sleep wouldn't claim him for hours.

CHAPTER FIFTEEN

NICK WOULD HAVE LEFT at first light, but hard rains had kept him pinned in the barn until almost nine o'clock. As soon as the sky cleared, he headed for the corral. He'd stayed clear of the cabin. There seemed to be no need to say goodbye to anyone.

Mike and Annie would be happy to see him go— there'd be no tearful goodbyes with them. And Ellie, well, they'd said all that needed to be said yesterday. And, in truth, he wasn't sure if he had the strength to say goodbye to her.

The idea of leaving her saddened him beyond words, but it was best to make a clean break now. He'd see she got the reward money and that she and Rose would be taken care of.

Nick was draping his saddle blanket over his mare's back when an old man rode up to the coach stop on a gray gelding. Drenched, he wore black and sported a white beard that grew into a point.

The stranger rode toward the corral and dismounted. He shook the rain from his hat. "You the groom?"

Nick turned toward his saddle, hanging over the fence. "Nope."

"A guest?"

"Not exactly."

"Ah, not an employee and not a guest. A man who defies description."

The hint of humor in the newcomer's voice had Nick smiling despite his foul mood. "Something like that."

The other man didn't press. He placed his hands at the base of his spine and arched his back. "There was a time I could ride for days and feel just fine. Now I've got to stop every half day to stretch my legs and empty my bladder. Getting old is a damnable curse."

Nick glanced down at the stranger. Despite his complaints, his eyes were bright. "My name is Nick Baron."

The old man held out his hand. "Reverend Shaun Johnson. I've come here to marry Annie and Mike."

Nick nodded. "They are expecting you." He felt cut off, out of touch with news in the area. Frank Palmer could be over the rise, for all he knew. "I've been here over a week. Pick up any news in the area?"

The minister shrugged. "No more than the usual. I hear from a couple of cowhands on the trail that they captured a fellow a few days' ride from here. He's wanted for murder and a railroad robbery."

Nick's interest sharpened. "He got a name?"

"They say it's Palmer. But you never can tell. When the reward is high, folks would turn their mother in to the jailhouse."

Damn, could it be that easy? Could it be over with Frank? He felt no relief, only an anxious need to see Frank face-to-face. "Where they taking him?"

"Word is Butte."

Butte. It made sense that Frank would be headed that way. Perhaps he'd figured out where the gold was without the map.

Nick put his saddle over the horse. He'd soon find out.

"You staying after the wedding?" he asked the minister.

"No. I've got to be moving on."

"Where you headed?"

"Butte, as a matter of fact."

"I'm heading in the same direction myself."

"If you wait until after the ceremony, I'll ride with you. The trail is a might more tolerable with company."

Nick wanted to get away from here while he still had the strength to leave Ellie. But as he looked at the old man's hands, bent by arthritis and time, he knew the pastor would fare better if he traveled with him. "How long you going to be?"

"An hour, maybe two. Just long enough to hitch these two folks and get me a bite to eat."

"A few more hours won't make a difference to me." If Frank was in jail, a day or two wouldn't make any difference. And he couldn't resist one last look at Ellie. "How about we leave at noon?"

"Sounds good to me."

Nick decided then that this hunger he had for Ellie had turned him into a fool. "Go on inside and I'll un-saddle your horse and turn him loose in the corral."

"Appreciate it. I hear Miss Annie has hired a new cook who cooks like an angel."

"Very true."

The minister hesitated a second as he looked at Nick. Recognition flickered in the pastor's eyes. "Have we met before?"

"No."

"But I have heard about you."

Tensing, Nick pulled the saddle off his horse and hung it on the corral fence again. "Most people have."

The pastor grinned. "Not all the stories were bad. I know a family that was brutalized by that outlaw Ramsey. The little girl didn't start sleeping at night until you locked that outlaw up in jail."

The information caught Nick by surprise. He never looked back after a job or stopped to think how his actions affected others.

Reverend Johnson laid his hand on Nick's arm. "You're an avenging angel," the minister said. "And a real blessing to many people."

Nick felt his throat tighten. An unseen weight lifted from his shoulders. Perhaps he was still one of the good guys. "That's a first for me."

"You've done more good than you realize."

Nick nodded. "Good to know."

"Well, let me get some breakfast so we can get this marriage ceremony going." The old man walked inside the house.

Nick stayed with the horses. He unsaddled the pastor's horse and took the blanket off his own. Like it or not, he'd be here for a few more hours.

He heard the women greet the minister. Ellie's voice mingled with Annie's. It bothered him that the last time he'd seen Ellie, she'd had red-rimmed eyes. Her pale face would haunt him for years to come.

Nick sighed. There was no changing the truth. He loved Ellie.

ELLIE WAS SURPRISED when Nick didn't leave, and secretly glad. However she kept her emotions in check. The reverend had said Nick had agreed to wait so that they could travel together. Ellie did her best not to read any more emotion into Nick's action.

Reverend Johnson's easy manner and kindness helped ease her frayed nerves. She liked the old man. He possessed a youthful spirit.

As the minister ate, the sun broke through the lingering clouds. By the time he'd finished his coffee, the sky was clear, as though it had never rained. Annie and Mike could be married outside after all, just as they'd hoped.

The minister and Mike left the cabin so that Ellie could help Annie dress in a lovely yellow calico that set off her blond hair and blue eyes just right. She fixed Annie's hair in a neat chignon that accentuated her high cheekbones.

Annie sat fidgeting with the trim on her cuff as Ellie fed and changed Rose. By the time she was done, there was barely time to brush her own hair and dust the flour from the skirts of the store-bought blue calico. She'd loved to have taken more time with her appearance, especially since Nick was staying for the ceremony. But the time simply wasn't there.

As she headed toward the door with Rose, she took one last glance at the wedding cake, which sat in the middle of the table. The two-tiered cake was adorned with fresh white and blue flowers. Around it, newly scrubbed plates, dishes and spoons waited for the guests. Fresh coffee simmered on the stove.

Everything was perfect.

Almost.

"Ladies," the minister called. "We're ready for you."

Annie stood at the threshold of the front door, her eyes wide. "This is it."

Ellie, with the baby on her shoulder, smiled. "You look lovely."

Annie smoothed her hands over her dress. "Do you think so? I feel kinda foolish dressed like this. I'm used to my buskins and chaps. Mike picked the dress out for me while we were in town."

She'd never seen her friend so nervous. "It looks lovely. You look lovely."

"I never thought that I would be so agitated when we got married. I mean, we made our pledge in front of my father's people and, well, we've shared blankets. It's not like there are any surprises left."

Ellie envied her friend. She was marrying the man she loved. "I think every time we pledge our love, we open ourselves up. A marriage ceremony, no matter how many times it's done, is much the same."

She swallowed. "I've never been good about speaking my emotions."

Ellie look Annie's hand in hers. Despite the warm day, her fingers were as cold as ice. "It's okay."

Annie lifted her shoulders. "I think the menfolk are getting impatient."

"Then let's not keep them waiting."

The women moved outside to the front porch.

Annie's gaze went directly to Mike. Ellie's gaze went to Nick, who stood by the corral.

His eyes were partially shadowed by the brim of his hat, but she could see that he was staring at her. His gaze traveled over her like a caress. Every muscle in her body quivered. She wanted nothing more than to reach out to him. Sadly, there was no going back.

Her throat felt raw as she faced Annie and Mike.

The minister held a large book. Its black leather was well worn, the spine cracked in two places. The book flopped opened directly to the marriage ceremony.

He peered over his glasses at Mike and Annie. "Ready?"

Mike squeezed Annie's hand. "We are."

In the background, majestic mountains touched a crystal-blue sky. A gentle breeze brushed the tall grass. It was a perfect day.

Annie smiled up at Mike. "Yes, we are."

Ellie patted Rose on the back. They couldn't have chosen a more beautiful day to marry, she thought.

"Dearly beloved, we are gathered here today to

join this man and woman." The minister's deep voice floated over Ellie's head. There'd been a few fleeting moments when she'd pictured herself standing in front of a minister with Nick at her side. The fact that she never would broke her heart.

Rose started to fuss and she shifted the baby to her other shoulder. She'd love to slip away from this ceremony and have a good cry.

"I do," Mike said.

His clear, strong voice brought Ellie back to the moment. She blinked away tears and watched as Annie recited her vows.

Suddenly she was aware that Nick was standing directly behind her. She sniffed, praying she'd not blubber like a fool and make a spectacle of herself. He placed his hands on her shoulders. Her muscles tensed. Then the warmth of his fingers seeped into her, dashing away all the fear and the tension.

He pressed his lips close to her ear. "Marry me."

She didn't dare look at him. But her body was very aware of him. His touch. His scent. The rise and fall of his chest.

The minister completed the ceremony and pronounced Annie and Mike husband and wife. Only when the newlyweds kissed did Ellie turn around and look up into Nick's eyes.

"You said you never wanted to see me again," she said.

He sighed. "I was angry. And I also said hurtful things. I am sorry."

"We both made mistakes."

He squeezed her shoulders. "Marry me," he said again. "Let us build a life together."

She stared, shocked by his proposal. "What about Frank and the gold?"

"I'll have to deal with both. We'll have no peace until that problem is resolved. But after I am done with him, it'll be just you, me and Rose." He cupped the child's small head in his large hand. "I'll be a good father to her."

Tears did stream down her face at that. "Nick, are you really sure about this? I lived at the Silver Slipper all my life. People don't think the best of me for it."

"We're making a fresh start here. The past doesn't matter."

She hugged him close. "I will make you a good wife, I swear."

He kissed her on the lips. He tasted so good.

Nick pulled away from Ellie with some effort. "Reverend Johnson."

The old man, who'd been talking to Annie and Mike, looked at him with expectant eyes. "Yes?"

"We got one more ceremony for you to perform."

The minister grinned. He reached into his breast pocket and retrieved his book.

Annie and Mike looked shocked.

"Are you sure about this, Ellie?" Annie asked, going to her.

Ellie glanced up at Nick. Her heart swelled with love. "Never more sure of anything in my life."

Annie shook her head as she met Nick's gaze. "Oh, this mothering business is more upsetting than I thought. Take good care of my girls, Mr. Baron, or my Arapaho brothers and I will hunt you down."

Nick nodded, his eyes full of respect.

Ellie felt mortified. And loved and cherished by Annie. No one had cared about her like this before.

The minister turned back the pages of his book. "Well, let's get started."

Nick took Rose from Ellie and laid the child on his shoulder. The baby cooed and sucked her fist. He patted her on the back. Ellie knew then that she'd never love another man like she loved Nick Baron.

"Dearly beloved, again," the minister said, smiling. "We are gathered here on this glorious day to join Nick and Ellie in holy matrimony."

Nick wrapped his hand around Ellie's. Warmth and a sense of security radiated through her body. She'd never seen a man more handsome.

It didn't matter that her dress wasn't fine or that he wore mud-splattered chaps. She didn't need special lace or a white dress. Nick was all she wanted.

"Do you, Nick, take Ellie to be your wife?" the minister asked.

"I do," he said in a confident voice.

Ellie's heart swelled. Annie sniffed back a tear as Mike wrapped his arm around his new wife.

"Ellie, do you take Nick as your husband?"

"I do." Lord, but her heart felt as if it would burst. Ellie would be a good wife to Nick. She swore it to herself and before God.

There were no rings to be exchanged. The minister declared them husband and wife.

Nick didn't hesitate. He faced Ellie and leaned forward. Gently he kissed her on the lips. "We will make a fine team, you and I. It will be good between us."

"I know."

They all retired to the house. Ellie laid a sleeping Rose in her cradle. Nervous excitement bubbled inside her as she moved into the kitchen to eat the luncheon she'd prepared. She had outdone herself with the offering for her friend's wedding. She'd put so much love and care into its making, never realizing that the cake would also celebrate her own marriage.

"The cake is so lovely," Annie said. "You've a gift with food, Ellie."

"You make cooking sound special. It's not."

Annie shook her head, her eyes quite serious. "You nurture the soul. Your cooking brings happiness and life to an otherwise sad and lonely house."

Nick wrapped his arm around her. "My wife doesn't know her value."

Ellie felt herself blushing. She wondered how she'd ever get through the meal. Her stomach was full of butterflies and her body sang with a restless energy.

The five sat down to the table filled with breads, jams, roasted chicken and cured ham. The group savored the meal, a rare treat by Montana standards. The reverend talked of his travels and some of the weddings he had performed. Mike offered up stories of his own. He had traveled the state from tip to tip and had met countless people.

Nick, however, was quiet. He would often take Ellie's hand in his or smile down at her. But he seemed to have no desire to join the conversation.

Ellie's mind moved to what would happen when they were alone this evening. She had grown up around women who traded their bodies for money. She certainly understood what happened in the bedroom, yet she was painfully aware now of her limited experience. It was one thing to *hear* about something and quite another to *do* it.

The group lingered around the table until well past the noon hour. It was the minister who finally rose.

He patted his full belly. "If I don't get on the trail now, I won't make it to my next stop before dark. I regret that I have lost my traveling companion, but I can think of no better reason."

Nick stood. "If you wait a day, I will ride with you to Butte. I still have unfinished business there."

Ellie glanced up at Nick. She'd forgotten all about Frank and the gold. Nick had not.

"I'd promised an old friend I'd be there by Saturday."

"He can surely wait an extra day," Annie said. "Stay and enjoy this lovely day."

"You tempt me, ma'am, but I must be on my way. My friend is a worrier by nature and I fear he will send the sheriff out looking for me if I do not head out."

"But it is only a day," Annie said.

He took Annie's hand in his. "I have traveled this state since you were a babe. This journey will be simple, like the thousand before it. Besides, two young couples should enjoy their privacy. The world offers precious little of it."

Nick frowned. "I promised to travel with you."

"Sir, you will not join me now. Enjoy your new wife."

"I will catch up to you on the trail," Nick said.

Ellie held her breath. She didn't want Nick to leave her ever. Let Frank have his gold.

The minister laughed. "Mr. Baron, do not be in such a rush to catch up to an old man when you have such a lovely wife."

As the minister walked away, Nick turned to Mike. "I don't want to leave at all. But Frank must be drawn out. And the best way to do that is to get the gold."

Mike stood. "Nick, if you don't mind, I'll ride with you tomorrow. Annie has told me about your trip and it seems to me an extra hand and gun could be helpful."

Nick hesitated. Ellie sensed that he'd always worked alone and that accepting help from anyone was a challenge for him. He nodded. "Appreciate it."

Within a half hour the minister sat astride his horse. Tied to his saddle was a sack of leftover food from the meal. Ellie had seen to it that he would eat well for days.

They all bid the old man goodbye. The couples remained on the front porch watching until the preacher was nearly out of sight. Ellie was glad for the quiet moment. She was in no rush to let go of her new husband.

When they could delay no more, each turned to the chores that needed doing even on a wedding day.

Horses demanded feeding, vegetables had to be picked and wagon wheels were in need of repair.

Ellie didn't see much of Nick for the rest of the day. Though the chores kept her hands busy, her mind returned over and over again to the night. After tonight, she and Nick would be bonded forever.

As the sun started to dip, Ellie finished washing the dinner plates. Nick and Mike had gone to the barn to bed the animals down for the night. She nursed Rose and changed her diaper. Annie dried the last of the dishes.

"I'm going to visit the necessary," Annie said.

Ellie nodded. "Take a lantern."

Alone in the cabin, Ellie felt the weight of the coming night on her shoulders. She glanced toward her room. Through the half-open door, she could see the bed.

Ellie glanced up, shocked to see Nick standing on the threshold. Again he'd sneaked up on her without her hearing. "I swear I am going to tie a bell around your neck."

Even, white teeth flashed. "I will try to move more loudly from now on." He opened his arms to her and she went to them without hesitation. Wrapped in his embrace, she felt safe.

Her heart tripped. "Annie said the baby could stay upstairs with her tonight."

"For this night only. After this, she stays with us. She is our girl."

Tears filled her eyes. "There are things I should tell you about myself, Nick," she said.

"They don't matter, Ellie. What matters is this day forward."

Talking to him about something as intimate as her virginity overwhelmed her with embarrassment. "I don't want to disappoint you tonight."

"You won't."

She couldn't bring herself to say the words. "I will make you happy, Nick."

He took her hand in his. "You already do."

CHAPTER SIXTEEN

ELLIE FOLLOWED NICK to her room. Her window was open and a warm breeze blew through it. Outside, a thousand stars twinkled in the sky. She paused by the window. "Have you ever made a wish on a star?"

He glanced up at the sky. A faint smile touched his lips. "No."

She tucked a curl behind her ear. "I've done it a million times. Every clear night I could get away from the Silver Slipper, I'd sneak outside. I'd get as far away from the music and laughter as I could. And then I'd look up into the sky and wish."

"What did you wish for?"

She hesitated. She'd never spoken of her starlight wishes to anyone. "There were times I wished my ma was alive. There were other times when I wished I could go to school with the other children. But mostly I wished that I'd have someone to love me."

He pulled her into an embrace. He hugged her

tight and in that moment all the lonely nights she'd ever spent vanished.

"We are lucky to have found each other, Ellie." His voice was tight with emotion. "It will be good between us."

No words of love. But for Ellie, it was enough for now.

He kissed her tenderly, then led her to the bed. Moonlight steamed in through the open window and shone onto her bed. The blankets had been folded down. Beside the bed sat Nick's saddlebag. His book rested on the bedside table. Already, he'd made the space his own. He'd only been in her life a very short time, and he'd already made a mark on her forever.

Ellie's stomach twisted as she stared at the bed. Nick laid his hands on her shoulders. She nearly jumped out of her skin. He chuckled. "You're nervous."

"Yes." She looked up at him.

Gently he fingered her collarbone with his thumb. Desire burned in his eyes. He reached for the top button of her bodice and unfastened the first three. He kissed the soft skin at the base of her throat. She hissed in a breath. Bolts of desire shot through her. She threaded her fingers through his hair and lifted his face. She kissed him on the lips, savoring his taste.

Nick smiled. "We'll not rush this moment. I want to savor every inch of you."

The heat inside of her nearly exploded. Her body throbbed for him.

He smiled as if he read the lust in her eyes. With painstaking slowness, he unfastened three more buttons. The curve of her breasts swelled over the top of her chemise. He kissed each mound and nibbled gently at the tender skin.

Ellie reached for the remaining buttons of her bodice and unfastened them to her waist. Nick pushed her bodice off her shoulders and past her hips. The dress dropped to the floor. The cool evening air brushed her warm skin.

He stared down at her breasts as they rose and fell. Her nipples puckered and strained against the thin fabric of her chemise. Her breath grew shallow.

She reached between her breasts for the faded pink ribbon tied into a neat bow. She tugged it free. Her chemise slipped off her shoulder. Nick kissed that bare shoulder as he cupped a taut breast in his hand.

"You taste sweet and salty at the same time."

She chuckled, marveling in her womanly powers. "Salt balances the sweet and makes it more flavorful."

He removed her chemise. She stood in front of

him, naked from the waist up. He caught a nipple in his calloused hand and then lowered his mouth to it. He suckled, teasing the tender pink flesh with his teeth.

Ellie felt an ache at her very core. She yearned for him to be inside her and to give her the climax she'd heard so much about. But as much as she wanted the release, she also wanted to savor this moment as long as she could.

She cupped his face in her hands and brought it up to her face. She kissed him on the lips and smiled. "Now, it is my turn."

Ellie was all bravado, but this all felt so natural and right, and that knowledge made her bolder than she'd ever dared dream she could be. She unfastened the buttons of his shirt and then pulled it over his head. Dark chest hair blanketed his broad chest. Her boldness seemed to shock and please him.

She took the same path he had. First, she kissed the hollow of his neck and then she began to trail kisses down his chest. She captured his nipple between her lips and worked her tongue around the tender flesh.

Nick hissed in a breath. "If you keep that up, this will go much faster than I'd planned."

The strain in his voice made her smile. She pulled away from his chest and circled his wet nipple with her thumb. Growing up in a brothel did have some advantages. She knew how to satisfy a man. And she intended to give all she had to Nick.

Her gaze locked on his stormy eyes and she reached for his belt buckle. With deliberate slowness, she unfastened the belt loop. He sucked in his flat belly as her knuckles grazed his skin. She undid the top button and then the second.

He captured her hand and banded his arms around her, crushing her breasts against his chest. He kissed her deeply, longingly, as if trying to regain a handle on his fragile control. He gripped her buttocks and pressed her against his hardness.

She slid her hand down the back of his pants and squeezed his tight buttocks.

In that instant, whatever hold he had on his control snapped. He lifted her up and she wrapped her legs around his waist. He carried her to the bed and laid her in the center. He loomed over her, his dark gaze burning into her skin, and then he reached for the hem of her skirt and pulled it up to her waist.

Through her pantaloons he pushed the heel of his hand against her moist center. Her throat went dry. She had never known such intense wanting. She pushed her hips up, pushing into his hand.

Nick stepped back and yanked down his pants, not bothering to take them completely off. She kept her gaze locked on his, not daring to look at his hard sex, fearing she'd lose her nerve. So far, instinct and second-hand knowledge had driven her to be bold. Now, she knew she was out of her depth.

She did not need to worry. Nick worked his knees between her thighs and pressed them open. He pushed the tip of his penis between the slit of her pantaloons and positioned it against her. Ellie opened her legs wider.

In one thrust, Nick pushed inside her. A wave of pain rocked Ellie's body. Every muscle tensed and for a moment she couldn't breathe.

ELLIE was a virgin!

The realization sliced through Nick's brain.

Every one of his muscles urged him to seek his release. She was so tight, so lovely and so moist. But the desire that had driven her had been doused by pain.

Nick remained inside of her but he didn't move so that she could adjust to him. He kissed her closed eyes. "Give your body time." His voice was a hoarse whisper and he barely recognized it.

"I didn't know it would hurt so."

"The pain will fade quickly." Nick licked his fingers and began to slowly rub circles around the tip of her womanhood, now swollen with desire.

A soft sigh escaped her lips and, slowly, the tension in her body began to ease.

"Better?" he whispered in her ear.

"Yes," she said, a bit breathless.

He waited for her to become more comfortable. "Does it feel good?"

"Yes."

Her honesty stoked his heat. Most women would have blushed or shrank away in shame, but Ellie didn't deny herself these earthy pleasures.

Gently he began to move inside her. At first she tensed as if she expected another wave of pain, but when none seemed to come, she relaxed. His circles grew tighter and he pressed harder.

Ellie lifted her hips. A moan rumbled in her throat.

His own desire, which he'd barely been able to restrain, broke free. He began to move in and out of her in a rhythm that was as old as time.

Ellie bit her bottom lip. "I don't know what I'm feeling."

"Do you like it?"

"Yes. But I want…*more.*"

Sweat damped his back. "Then you shall have your release." He moved faster, holding off his own pleasure until she found hers.

Then, suddenly, her body tensed. The muscles in her neck strained as she arched her head back. He savored the raw pleasure on her face. When she called out his name and gripped his back, he drove into her one last time, allowing himself his own release.

Nick was certain his heart stopped for a moment as the pleasure seized him. He collapsed against Ellie, resting his face in the crook of her neck. Sweat mingled between their half-dressed bodies. Their heartbeats thrummed in a wild rhythm.

Slowly, his mind cleared and reason returned. "Ellie?"

She drew small, lazy circles on his back with her fingers. "Hmm?"

"You were a virgin."

"I know."

He hoisted himself up on his elbow. Her eyes were closed and a satisfied smile curled the edges of her lips. "Why didn't you tell me?"

She opened her eyes. Desire still lingered in her gaze. "You said we were starting over and that the past didn't matter."

He stroked her cheek. "But if I'd known, I would have gone slower…taken more time."

"If you'd taken any more time, I think I might have exploded."

He frowned. "I was too rough."

"You were wonderful."

He captured a piece of her skirt between his fingers. "I'd have at least undressed you properly."

She chuckled. "You can still do that."

He ran his hand up her leg. Damn, but he was growing hard again. "Aren't you sore?"

She stroked his buttocks. "Not really. Should I be?"

"Hell, I don't know. I've just heard that women needed a rest after." His late wife had begged a week's respite from his advances. "How did you manage to stay a virgin?"

"Miss Adeline didn't pay much attention to me when I was little. I was a scrawny child with wild red hair, so she put me to work in the kitchen. And I know there were times when I got older that Miss Adeline wanted to put me to work, but Chin Lo said he would quit if he didn't have me as his assistant. She needed Chin Lo more than she needed another working girl, so she never crossed him."

"I thought you two were lovers."

"Chin Lo and me? No. He treated me like his child."

"I'm truly indebted to the man for keeping you safe."

She sighed. "I knew my days were numbered after he died. It was a matter of time before she put me to work upstairs. Even then, I couldn't seem to find the courage to leave. Then Rose was born and I knew I couldn't stay."

He kissed her on the shoulder. It was a miracle she had survived at all. He was so thankful she'd been spared the upstairs rooms. "You should rest."

"I can rest later." Her voice had grown husky. "I'm anxious to show you a few things I learned at the Silver Slipper."

He lifted a brow. "You learned things?"

"Mind you, I've no practical experience, but the girls talked and shared some of their secrets. I must admit that I'm anxious to try a few of those ideas out on you."

He chuckled as he rubbed his hand under her skirt and up her naked thigh. "Like what?"

A faint blush colored her cheeks. She tracked her fingertip over his flat belly and then to his open belt and pants. "Well, I'm not very good at talking about such things. But I can show you."

Nick grew hard. Ellie had the power to drive him insane. He sucked his breath when her hand slid into his pants. Her fingers circled around his manhood.

And she spent the next hour showing him what she couldn't put into words.

WHEN ELLIE WOKE, the sun was streaming into the room. Nick's naked body was spooned against her buttocks and his hand curled around her breast. An undeniable sense of peace washed over her. Never in her life had she felt so safe and so wanted.

For the first time in her life, she did not fear tomorrow.

FRANK LIFTED his face to the bright, warm sun. His visit to the mining town had been downright pleasant. He'd had a bath and a good meal. The food wasn't as good as Ellie's and the cook wouldn't let him sit in the kitchen while she cooked, but it was all passable. He was more than ready to find his Ellie and his baby girl.

He shifted in his saddle and sucked in a deep breath. This was his favorite time of year. Traveling was easy, the night chill didn't keep him awake and the hunting was good.

Anticipation coursed through his veins. He was only a day's ride from the Spring Rock coach stop. Soon he'd find Ellie. Soon his life would be perfect.

Jade and Monty had thought they'd outsmarted him. That Jade was a sneaky bitch. If not for her meddling, he, Ellie and Monty would be in Missouri living on the farm he and his brother had always talked about owning.

Frank sighed.

Monty. Remorse swept over him as he thought

about the last terrified look in Monty's eyes. "Dumb son of a bitch."

Damn Jade.

There was no getting Monty back, but the rest of his family would soon be together again.

"I'm coming for you, Ellie," he said to the wind. His pure, sweet Ellie. "We're going to be together real soon."

CHAPTER SEVENTEEN

ELLIE WOULD HAVE loved to stay in bed with Nick all day. Her body still tingled from their lovemaking this morning, yet she already ached to touch him again.

But the day's chores and Rose would not be ignored. She and Nick reluctantly dressed and went outside.

They found Mike and Annie standing by the corral. "As much as I'd like to dally, Montana doesn't allow it," Mike said. Days off now would catch up to him when winter came.

Nick nodded. "I'll give you a hand with the horses." He kissed Ellie on the cheek and the two men headed to the barn.

A lazy smile curled the edges of Annie's mouth as she watched her husband walk toward the barn. "My husband does cut a nice figure."

Ellie laughed. "Where are the practical women who protected their hearts?"

Annie laughed. "They fell in love."

"Love does have a way of changing things, doesn't it?"

"Oh my, yes."

They both laughed and started inside the cabin. Ellie crossed the threshold as she had done a hundred times before. But this time the cabin seemed different. Oh, it was just as she'd left it yesterday. The stove still dominated the kitchen, the great stone chimney towered over the main room and even the bread she'd baked yesterday still sat on the kitchen table under a white-and-red-checked cloth. But it was *different*.

For the first time since she'd arrived at the coach stop, she didn't know what to do with herself. The house and kitchen didn't really feel like hers now. She didn't belong here anymore. She belonged with Nick—wherever that was.

"Why the worried expression?" Annie asked.

Ellie glanced up at her. "I'm not worried."

Annie moved to the stove. She set a pan of milk to warm and then poured two cups of coffee into twin mugs. "I've never seen a deeper frown. Was everything all right last night?"

Ellie sighed as she sat at the kitchen table. "I know I belong with Nick, but I don't know where we will go or where we will live. He has said he has land near here."

"Maybe I could answer that," said Nick.

Annie jumped. "The Indians were right. You move as silent as a ghost."

Ellie turned to see him standing in the doorway. The wind had tousled his hair and the top two buttons of his white shirt were unfastened. Her heart tripped. Lord, but the man had the power to turn her knees weak.

Nick strode into the room. "I thought you and I could take a ride today and have a look at our new home. Honestly, I don't know if the house on the site is livable."

Excitement welled in Ellie. "There is a house on the land?"

He nodded. "Brand-new. Never been lived in."

Her first real home. "I'd like to see the house."

Nick didn't take his gaze off Ellie. "Annie, would you mind watching our daughter today? We'll be back by supper."

Annie grinned as she took the baby from Ellie. "I can think of nothing else I'd rather do."

Ellie stood, smoothing her hands over her skirt. "It won't be any trouble, Annie?"

Annie nuzzled her face close to Rose's. "This little peanut is never any trouble."

"It's settled," Nick said. "I've saddled our horses and we can leave now."

Nervous excitement washed over Ellie. "Right now?"

"No time like the present."

Her brain raced. She wasn't even worried about riding on a horse. "I should pack us a basket of food."

He winked at her. "As soon as you are packed, we can leave."

TWO HOURS LATER, Nick and Ellie reached the ranch Bobby had left to Nick. Like Ellie, he was seeing the property for the first time. She was glad that he'd waited and they could share this moment.

Ellie shielded her eyes with her hand as she stared at the simple one-story house. The weather had mellowed the freshly milled wood to a dark brown. It wasn't big, but there was a wide front porch and windows on every side of the house.

They dismounted and walked to the cabin. A thick layer of dust covered the porch and the windows that flanked the front door were streaked with dirt.

"Doesn't look like Bobby spent much time here," Nick said.

Ellie pushed open the door. The hinges squeaked.

Sunlight seeped in through the grimy windows. Dust particles danced in faint bands of light across an empty room. Ellie pictured a large bed, Rose's cradle beside it, rugs to warm the floor and a big table that would one day be surrounded by their children.

Children.

Ellie's hand slid to her flat belly. She could already be carrying Nick's baby. If she were pregnant, the baby would be born in May. Spring. A good time for babies.

Ellie's gaze was drawn to the one bit of hardware in the room—the black cast-iron stove. She walked over to it. Except for the thick coat of dust, it was pristine. "This stove has never been used."

"Bobby always talked about marrying a woman who could cook anything. When we'd share a campfire on the trail, he'd go on and on about the dishes his wife would make him."

She opened the oven door and peered inside. "This cost him a pretty penny."

"The man took his food seriously."

She laughed as she stood. "What was his favorite food?"

Nick moved behind her and placed his hands on her shoulders. "He was partial to steak and fries, and he never said no to a chokeberry pie."

"Then that shall be the first meal I make."

Nick's eyes softened. "He'd appreciate that."

Her heart clenched as she looked up at him. She'd never get tired of looking at him. She took in a breath and surveyed the cabin. "I used to dream of having my own home. There are so many things I want to do here."

"Such as?"

"Curtains in the windows, a big feather bed, a large table where we can gather for meals. I suppose one day we might even add rooms onto the cabin."

"Children need lots of room."

Ellie's heart just about melted. "Brothers and sisters for Rose."

"I miss having a family. A house isn't right unless it's filled with children."

Under the words she sensed sadness. "Have you written to your family since you left Virginia?"

"Three times. I never heard back. They haven't forgiven me for what happened with Gregory."

"It's been ten years, Nick. You should try again. Didn't you say you had a sister you were fond of?"

"Julia. She was nine when I left."

"She is a grown woman now."

"I doubt she remembers me."

"You won't know unless you write her."

He inhaled a deep breath. "Here we are in our new home and the talk has turned sad. I don't want there to be sadness in this house today."

There was a wall around Nick's heart, but she sensed a tiny bit of it had started to crumble. Later, when they'd settled into the cabin, she'd bring up the letter again.

"So what are your plans for this house?" she asked. "I hope you intend to do more than help me make babies."

He chuckled. "Very tempting, but I was thinking about raising horses."

"No desire to pan for gold?"

"None. I've ridden this area enough to see that the veins are drying up. But men will always need horses. The railroad alone could keep me in business."

"You've thought this through."

"About a thousand times on the trails during the last year."

"We can get started right away."

"As much as I'd like to get started now, it's too late in the season to buy new animals. I'll have to buy what hay I need to feed my horse and a milk cow." He walked to the window and stared at the virgin lands. Wind washed over the tall grass like waves. "I'll start cutting wood right away and build corrals and maybe even a barn before the heavy snows set in. By spring, I'll be ready for the horses."

She walked up behind him and wrapped her arms around his waist. "It sounds like a wonderful plan."

He faced her. "Ellie, living out here won't be easy. There are going to be good years and bad."

"I'm not afraid of hard work, especially since I'm building a real home for the first time in my life."

He leaned forward and kissed her. She rose up on tiptoes, wrapped her arms around his neck and deepened the kiss.

A soft groan rumbled in Nick's chest. He pulled back. "If you don't stop that, Mrs. Baron, I won't be able to wait until we get back to Annie's."

"You've got a saddle blanket that you can spread on the floor."

"In broad daylight? I've married a wanton woman."

"Complaining?"

"Not in the least, lady. Not in the least."

He kissed her lightly and went to fetch the blanket. Five minutes later it was spread out on the floor. He sat on it and started to pull off his boots.

"In a bit of a rush, aren't you, Mr. Baron?" She started to unfasten the row of buttons that trailed between her breasts.

"I can think of no better way to christen our new cabin."

She shrugged off her bodice and laid it on the edge of the blanket. Her breasts peeked out over the top of her chemise. She reached for the pink bow between them.

Dark lust replaced the laughter in his eyes. "Come here, Mrs. Baron."

She'd learned from the girls at the Silver Slipper that anticipation was half the fun. Instead of going to him, she took a step back and slowly unlaced her shoes.

"Are you teasing me, woman?"

She let one shoe drop and then reached for the second set of laces. "I sure am."

Nick leaned back on his elbows, watching her as she set the second shoe aside. She reached for the button in the back of her skirt and unfastened it. The calico skimmed over her hips and fell into a puddle around her ankles. She undid the frayed cord that laced up her corset.

Nick rose up on his knees and took her hand in his. She was under him in an instant and he was pushing up the fabric of her chemise and kissing her breasts.

Ellie's playfulness vanished. She gave herself to the storm of desire that engulfed them both.

Much, much later, they lay together on the blanket, their clothes heaped together nearby. The sun had dipped. They had eaten their picnic lunch after they'd made love and then they'd made love again. The day had been perfect.

Nick sat up. "We best get back to Annie's."

Ellie stretched her arms high over her head. "I could stay here forever."

He kissed the tip of her naked breast. "We've got to get back. Rose will be looking for you." He handed her her chemise and pantaloons.

She sat up and started to dress. "Okay, we get Rose and then we come right back here."

He pulled up his pants. "With luck we can be back in a couple of weeks."

Disappointment washed over her. "That long?"

He yanked his shirt over his head, tucked it into his pants and fastened the buttons. "There's a lot to be done first."

"I know there will be supplies and furniture to be bought. I doubt we can afford much at first."

"Money's not a problem. About all I've done these last ten years is save what I made."

She pulled on her skirt and bodice. "Then there's nothing stopping us from setting up the house right away."

He put on his boots. "I've got to deal with Frank before we do anything here. The minister says there is a man in Butte who the authorities think is Frank."

Frank. He was a distant reminder of a nightmare she'd once lived. "Good, let him stay there."

He strapped on his gun. "I can't do that. I've got to see him for myself. And there is the matter of the gold. It has to be returned to the railroad."

"Can't we just forget the past?"

"Not this part of it." His voice had grown cold and hard.

"I have a bad feeling about this," she said.

He wrapped his arms around her. "Ellie, I'm very good at what I do. Even if the man they have isn't Frank, I will find him."

Her unease grew. She felt as if he were abandoning her. "You've never had anything to lose before."

"All the more reason to be very careful."

She could feel the glow of the day seeping from her bones. "Nick, please don't go."

He shook his head. "Ellie, you're not being fair. I have to go."

She pulled back. "Your life is not just about you anymore. There is Rose and me to consider."

"You knew from the start that I'd always go after Frank."

A cold shiver danced down her spine. "I don't want to lose you."

He cupped her face. "You won't."

Unshed tears choked her throat. "You have a responsibility to us."

"I have one to Bobby, too. The man was like a father to me. I could never make a life in the house he built if I didn't see his killer hang."

She knew she'd never change his mind, which

only stirred the anger and frustration inside her. "If you cared about me, you'd not go."

He pulled back. "That's not fair, Ellie."

"I don't care about fair anymore! I have a family now and I don't want to lose it."

He lifted his chin. "You've got to have a little faith in me."

"I *love* you," she said. Tears spilled down her face.

His eyes softened for a moment, but he said nothing. No words of love. No tender feelings. "I've got to get you back to Annie's."

The cold hard bounty hunter who had first appeared on her doorstep was back. Her loving husband was gone and she feared she'd never see him again. "If you leave, I can't guarantee Rose and I will be here when you get back."

Nick's scowl deepened. He strode out of the cabin, leaving Ellie to follow. She felt wretched as she climbed on her horse and the two rode back to Annie's in silence.

When they reached the coach stop, Ellie went inside the main cabin and fed Rose while Nick cared for the horses.

That night, Ellie went to bed in her room alone. She tossed and turned until well past midnight before an uneasy sleep claimed her.

In the darkness, Nick came to her. He slid into her

bed. He was naked. Neither spoke as he pushed up her nightgown. She opened her legs for him. He slid into her as if they'd made love a thousand times.

She put her heart and soul into their joining, matching his passion with her own. When they climaxed together, she spooned her body to his and he draped his arm over her waist. The warmth of his embrace soothed all her worries. Though they'd not spoken, she was confident their lovemaking had been apology enough to make up for all the terrible things she'd said.

In the morning, she vowed to tell him that she would always be here for him. Her anger had been born of fear. She just wanted him safe. He was her life now. And she would tell him again that she loved him.

As sleep overtook her, she vowed to make things all right when she woke.

THAT SAME NIGHT Reverend Johnson sat by his campfire, singing a hymn. The evening was warm and the breeze gentle. He'd eaten the delicious meal Ellie had made for him. Life didn't get much better.

He heard the snap of a twig and knew someone was behind him. He turned and saw a clean-shaven man with black hair and broad, muscular shoulders.

Over the years he'd stopped fearing strangers.

The Lord had sent all kinds his way. "Evening. Got a little coffee left in the pot if you'd like some."

The stranger nodded. "Much obliged." He sat across from the minister, pulled a tin cup from his saddlebag and poured his coffee. He sipped it. "Sure is good. Thanks."

"Name's Reverend Shaun Johnson."

"Frank."

The minister searched his mind. "Do I know you?"

Frank shook his head as he sipped his coffee. "Don't believe I've had the pleasure."

The reverend sat forward. He hated to judge a man before he got to know him, but there was something about this man that made the hairs on the back of his neck rise, as if Lucifer himself had come a calling.

Shaun decided to let the matter drop. He would tread lightly with this one. Likely he'd sleep with one eye open tonight. "So, where you headed?"

Frank's fingers tightened around his cup. "West."

No sin in being vague. "Me, I'm headed to Butte. Got friends there. You ever been there?"

"A time or two."

The two lapsed into silence. It was the minister's nature to chat but it was clear Frank wanted no part of talking.

"Don't suppose you have any grub to spare?" Frank said finally.

"Matter of fact I do. Got biscuits and a fine salty ham."

Frank accepted the fare and when he bit into the biscuit, his face softened. "Mighty tasty. Ain't often you get this kind of food out on the range."

"Got it from a coach stop not five hours west of here. A little redheaded cook by the name of Ellie made it for me."

Frank's eyes brightened. "That so?"

The reverend was pleased they had something to talk about. "Fact, I just married her to a nice fellow."

"You married her?" An edge had crept into his voice.

"To a fine man who will do right by her. He seems mighty smitten by her."

The stranger's hands curled into fists. "That baby of hers a girl?"

"Why, yes, she was. How'd you know?"

"Lucky guess. Where'd you say this coach stop was?"

"Five or six hours west, near the mouth of Thunder Canyon."

"Owned by a gal named Annie?"

"That's right."

"Appreciate the information." Frank pulled his gun and pointed it at the reverend. He fired.

The bullet struck the minister square in the chest by his heart. He fell back off the log he was sitting on and hit the dirt hard.

Pain seared through his chest and he couldn't catch his breath. He'd never expected to die on the side of the road. He'd always figured he'd die in town in a feather bed. He reckoned there was purpose in his death this fine evening, but he couldn't see it for the life of him.

Frank moved closer to the fire and squatted. He took what remained of the food Ellie had made. "My Ellie was always the best cook in the state."

It took all of Reverend Johnson's energy to focus.

Frank started to eat. "You had no right marrying them. Ellie is *my* wife."

CHAPTER EIGHTEEN

Nick was gone!

Ellie charged out of her room, buttoning her bodice as she hurried into the kitchen. No one. She ran outside, saw that Nick's horse was gone, and then hurried into the barn. No sign of Nick.

Running back to the cabin, she burst through the front door as Annie walked down the stairs. Rose was on her shoulder, sleeping.

"Nick's horse is gone!" Ellie said, breathless.

Annie nodded. "He and Mike left a couple of hours ago. They said they'd be back in a week or two."

Her shoulders slumped. "You should have woken me up."

"Nick said not to—that you needed your sleep."

"They've gone after Frank and the gold."

Annie laid Rose in the cradle in Ellie's room. "He knows what he's doing, Ellie. And Mike's handled his share of guns."

"I begged him not to go."

Annie shook her head. "He's got to put this matter to rest."

Ellie pressed her hands to her face. "I know he does."

"He will be all right," Annie said.

"I was horrible to him. I said terrible things. If anything should happen to him, I would die knowing the last words I said to him were so hateful."

Annie put her arm around Ellie's shoulder. "He will be fine."

Ellie wanted to believe Annie. But in her heart she feared she'd lost her only chance at love.

NICK AND MIKE saw the buzzards overhead at eleven o'clock in the morning. Something or someone ahead over the rise was dead or dying.

Mike shifted forward in his saddle. "We should check it out."

Nick didn't want to be gone from Ellie any longer than was necessary, but Mike was right. They had to check. "Yes."

Mike and Nick nudged their feet into their horses' haunches and climbed the rocky incline. When they reached the peak, Nick spotted the man lying on the ground. As they approached, he recognized the reverend instantly. Both men dismounted.

The minister lay on his back, his arms outstretched, his face turned toward the blistering sun. Blood oozed from a gash on his forehead.

Nick's gut clenched. He knelt beside the man. A bullet had seared through the left breast pocket of his coat, leaving a wide hole. No man could survive such a wound.

He closed his eyes and pinched the bridge of his nose, cursing himself for not making the man wait another day. "Damn."

Mike took off his hat. "The old man seemed unstoppable to me."

At the sound of Mike's voice, the minister stirred.

Startled, Nick glanced at Mike and then down at the old man. For the first time he saw the very shallow rise and fall of the reverend's chest.

"No man could survive a wound like that," Mike said.

"It won't be long before death comes," Nick said.

Nick shrugged off his range coat and covered the clergyman. At least he could keep him comfortable and give him a decent burial when it was over.

The minister shifted under the weight of the coat. "Tarnation, boy, I'm boiling as is," he gasped. "Your coat will cook me alive."

Nick snatched the coat back.

Mike laughed. "Reverend, you're talking mighty well for a man who's been shot through the heart."

The clergyman shifted and tried to sit up. Nick helped him. The old man's white hair stuck up from his head as if he'd grabbed hold of a telegraph wire. His nose was sunburned.

Reverend Johnson pulled a book from his breast pocket. A bullet was lodged in the center. "That's not important now."

Nick studied the quarter-size hole in Reverend Johnson's coat. "Begging your pardon, but you're one lucky man."

The minister grabbed Nick's arm. "Listen to me. A man named Frank Palmer shot me."

Nick stiffened. "Are you sure?"

"Very. And he's headed back toward the coach stop. Left early this morning. He is looking for Ellie. He said that she is *his* wife."

Nick's blood ran cold.

Mike paled. "The women are alone."

"Mike, stay with the reverend. We won't be able to move as fast with him. I'm headed back to the stop."

Mike's yes barely registered in Nick's mind. He was already running toward his horse.

Frank had a long lead on him. If Nick rode like hell, he could make up some of that, but he wasn't sure if it would be enough.

"Hold on, Ellie."

ELLIE SAW THE PLUME of dust on the horizon and her heart skipped. Nick! She stopped her butter churning and stood. Shielding her eyes with her hand, she watched. Seconds passed and though she couldn't see the rider's face, she realized the rider was too stocky to be Nick. Her heart sank. Another customer.

Wiping her hands on her apron, she called out to Annie. "We've got a guest coming."

Annie came out of the barn leading a gray sorrel into the corral. "Good. A customer will keep our minds off all the worrying we're both doing."

Ellie went inside, checked on the baby and then moved into the kitchen to check the stew she had simmering on the stove. She also had two pies cooling and bread ready for the oven. The guest would arrive to a feast.

She walked out to the front porch. The last thing she wanted to do now was to entertain a guest, but until she moved out of the stop, this was her job. And she owed Annie every day of work she could give her.

Annie walked toward the porch, wrapping a rope into a loop between her hand and elbow. She'd changed back into her customary garb of pants and a loosely fitting shirt. She'd twisted her golden curls into a tight braid that snaked down her back. "So, do we have anything to feed this fellow?"

The rider rode closer.

"A feast," Ellie said. "I wonder if I'll ever get in the habit of not cooking for a crowd."

Annie pulled off her hat and brushed the dust from the rim. "You and Nick will fill that house of yours up soon enough."

Children. The thought had her heart squeezing. *Be safe, Nick.*

She shifted her attention to the traveler, needing a distraction. Something seemed familiar about his build. His hat covered his hair and the brim shadowed his clean-shaven face.

It wasn't until the rider was nearly upon them that she realized who it was.

"Frank Palmer!" Ellie gasped.

Annie's eyes hardened into blue shards. Her father and her brothers had taught her to fight and she would fight Frank if need be. But Ellie worried she would die in a fight with Frank.

Ellie's heart lurched. "Annie, get inside!"

Annie did go inside, only to return seconds later with her shotgun—the very gun Ellie had shot Nick with. But before she could raise it, Frank pulled his pistol and fired.

The bullet grazed Annie's right temple and knocked her to the ground.

Ellie dropped to her knees. "Annie!" The older woman's eyes were closed, but she moaned at the sound of her name. The bullet had torn the skin at her temple but had not entered it.

Frank held up his hands. "There ain't no reason to be afraid, Ellie. It's me, Frank."

Ellie stiffened, glancing up. "You shot her!"

He replaced his gun. "She was gonna shoot me. I couldn't have that."

"Ellie," Annie muttered.

Ellie's eyes brimmed with tears and she dabbed Annie's temple with the corner of her apron. Annie would have a headache that would keep her flat on her back for a couple of days, but she'd survive—if Ellie could get them through this.

Frank touched the brim of his hat. "I been looking for you for a good while, girl. You're hard to find."

She held her apron corner to Annie's temple. "I thought you were in jail in Butte."

He looked surprised. "Nope. I guess they got the wrong fellow."

"I don't have the map, Frank."

Frank grinned. "You never was one to beat around the bush. I always liked that about you."

Ellie swallowed. "Nick Baron—the bounty hunter—has it. He's gone to Butte to dig the gold up and see who is in the jail. He'll be back any hour now."

Frank laughed as he dismounted. "The gold is in

Butte? Damn, it would be like Jade to hide it right under my nose." His spurs jangled as he approached the front porch. "Well, I see no reason to rush off, seeing as that bounty hunter is fetching my gold."

Ellie struggled to keep her voice even. "But he doesn't know you are here." She remembered their argument. "He might not come back."

"Oh, I think he'll be coming back. He'll figure out that fellow in the jailhouse ain't me and he'll come running back to you." Frank clapped his hands together. "In the meantime, I could use a good meal." He sniffed the air. "Is that stew I smell?"

Annie struggled to sit up. "You won't eat in my house, you—"

Ellie laid her hand on Annie's mouth, silencing her. If Miss Adeline had taught her anything, it was how to handle difficult men. "It sure is," she said, smiling. If Nick were coming back, she'd have to buy them as much time as she could. "Come on in and take a load off."

The happiness and relief on Frank's face were almost palpable. "And how is that baby girl of mine?" he said. "I bet she is growing like a weed."

Ellie choked back her fear. "She sure is." She helped Annie to her feet. She prayed she could stall Frank long enough to figure out how she was going to get herself out of this mess.

Two hours later Frank sat at the kitchen table, his hand on his round, taut belly. "I swear, Ellie, you are still the best cook in the state. I'll bet you'd give the girls back in Missouri a run for their money."

Ellie stood by the stove, her hands clenched. Annie sat in a chair that Frank had tied her to. Her head bandaged, she was fully awake. She strained at the ropes at her wrist but had not succeeded in loosening them. Ellie had warned her to keep silent. Annie had, but her blue eyes burned with a warrior's anger.

This last couple of hours had been the longest of Ellie's life. Frank had wanted to see the baby, but Ellie had convinced him to let the girl sleep. He'd been hungry enough to agree.

But now that he'd eaten three bowls of stew and had his fill of wedding cake, he was ready to visit.

"Missouri?" Ellie said. She picked up his dirty plate and scraped the leftovers into a slop bucket.

He scratched his beard. "I must have told you about Missouri. Lord knows we spent enough time together at the Silver Slipper."

He'd sat in the kitchen for hours staring at her, but he'd never spoken to her. "Tell me again. You know how I like to hear about it."

He grinned. "There's a farm near St. Louis that I've had my eye on since I was a boy. I figured we'd buy it and make it our home—you, me and the baby. What you say her name was?"

"Rose."

He wrinkled his nose. "I don't like that name. I've always been partial to Carol Sue. What do you think?"

Annie sucked in a sharp breath but she said nothing.

Ellie swallowed fear and anger. "It's a fine name."

"Well, from now on the baby's gonna be called Carol Sue. Carol Sue Palmer. I like the sound of that."

Ellie remembered the bruises on Jade's arms and knew Monty could be cruel. She suspected Frank wasn't much different. "Sounds good," she told Frank.

Nick, please come soon!

Frank picked his teeth with his pinky nail. "I met a friend of yours on the road."

Ellie froze. "You did?"

"The reverend. He told me you married the bounty hunter."

She didn't want to make Frank angry. But she'd not deny her marriage, either. "Yes."

"I wasn't happy about it. Lost my temper with the minister, as a matter of fact."

Ellie glanced at Annie. The woman's eyes reflected the worry and sorrow in her own heart. "But as I rode alone for a while, I cooled off. I figured this marriage problem of yours could be easily fixed. Once that bounty hunter shows up with the gold, I'll kill him."

It took everything in Ellie not to scream in panic.

He grinned. "Then we can live happily ever after."

Rose woke up and started to cry.

NICK SPOTTED Annie's stone house just before three o'clock in the afternoon. He was a good quarter of a mile away when he dismounted behind a stand of trees.

He'd made it to the coach stop in record time—four hours. He'd ridden his horse hard, as if Satan himself nipped at his heels. The mare was coated in a white lather and was breathing hard. She needed a rubdown but he didn't have the time. He pulled the saddle off his horse and turned her loose.

He moved to the edge of the trees and studied the house and surrounding buildings. A new horse was in the corral. Gray with white spots, the horse ate hay greedily from the bin as if it hadn't eaten in weeks. There was no sign of Ellie, Annie or Frank.

He wished like hell it was nighttime. He could use the darkness to his advantage. But sunset wouldn't come for hours and he feared what Frank would do to the women in that time.

Removing his rifle from his saddle, he checked his ammunition and started toward the cabin.

As he moved closer, he heard Rose's cry. Every muscle in his body tensed and it took everything in him not to rush the cabin.

"Enough's enough," Frank shouted from inside the cabin. "Shut that baby up!"

Nick sneaked up to the side window and pressed his body against the side of the house.

"I'm doing the best I can," Ellie shouted. The fear in her voice sliced through his heart.

Nick peeked in the window. Ellie held Rose close while Frank stood over her, his hand on his gun. Annie sat tied to a chair, straining to break her ropes. Blood soaked a bandage on her head.

"Babies ain't supposed to make such a ruckus," Frank said.

"She's not feeling well. She's cutting teeth!" Ellie cried.

"It's that tainted blood from her whore mother," Frank said. "Jade never knew when to shut up, either."

Ellie hugged the baby closer.

Frank looked ready to snap. "If she don't stop, I'm liable to put a bullet in her."

"No!" Ellie shouted. "You can't do that!"

Frank's eyes narrowed. "Now don't you be telling me what I need to do. You're *my* wife and I am the head of our household."

Fear tightened Ellie's face. "Please, Frank, this is no way to treat your little girl."

For a moment his face softened, but Rose's cries triggered fresh anger. "If she can't be quiet, I'll be teaching her a lesson."

"She's a baby!"

"Born to that bitch-whore Jade. We might have to go it without her, Ellie."

"Please, Frank, I love her."

"Your duty is to me. Now make that brat shut up or I'm killing it."

Nick hurried to the front door. He glanced in. He could see Frank and Ellie's shadows on the wall but he didn't have a clear shot.

"Let me give the baby to Annie," Ellie suggested. "We'll go outside where it's cool. You just need a moment's peace and then you will be fine."

Frank hesitated and then nodded.

"I'll need to untie Annie so she can care for the baby."

"No. Just lay the baby down on the floor in front of her. That brat can scream herself hoarse as long as I don't have to listen to her."

Nick pulled his gun and retreated to the side of the house once again.

Ellie and Frank moved outside. Frank slammed the cabin door closed. The distant drone of Rose's cries could still be heard.

Nick cocked his rifle, ready to fire, but Ellie stood between him and Frank.

Frank grabbed Ellie by the arm and pulled her against him. "Tell me you love me," he said.

Ellie's face was only inches from Frank's. Her auburn braid snaked down her back, teasing the top of her narrow waist. "I can't."

He twisted her arm. "Why not!"

She cried out in pain. "I love Nick."

Nick's heart twisted.

"He's the past," Frank said. "I am the future. Tell me you love me!"

"I can't!"

Frank's face turned red with rage. He slapped Ellie. The force of the blow knocked her to the ground.

Nick didn't hesitate. He fired. His bullet struck Frank in the chest, knocking him backward off the porch and into the dirt. He was dead.

Ellie screamed and scrambled away from Frank.

Nick went to her and cradled her in his arms. "Ellie, are you all right?"

She clung to him. "Nick! Thank God! I'm so sorry!"

"For what, darlin'?" The sadness in her voice shattered his heart.

She lifted her tear-streaked face up to his. "I was so hateful to you before you left. I love you."

"Ellie, I know that." He wiped a tear from her cheek with a gloved finger. "I'm the one who should be begging forgiveness. I love you so much and I never told you."

Tears streamed down her face as the baby's cries rushed out of the cabin.

He smiled. "Let's go inside and get our daughter before she shatters Annie's eardrums."

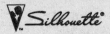

SPECIAL EDITION™

Go on an emotional journey in the next
book in

Marie Ferrarella's

miniseries

THE CAMEO

Don't miss:

SHE'S HAVING A BABY

Available October 2005
Silhouette Special Edition #1713

Left heartbroken and pregnant,
MacKenzie Ryan scoffed at her best friend's
suggestion she wear the legendary cameo
that paired the wearer with her true love in
one day's time...until she slipped it on and
Dr. Quade Preston moved in next door!
Could the legend of love be real?

Available at your favorite retail outlet.

Where love comes alive™

SAGA

National bestselling author

Debra Webb

A decades-old secret threatens to bring
down Chicago's elite Colby Agency in
this brand-new, longer-length novel.

COLBY
CONSPIRACY

While working to uncover the truth behind
a murder linked to the agency, Daniel Marks
and Emily Hastings find themselves trapped
by the dangers of desire—knowing every
move they make could be their last....

Available in October,
wherever books
are sold.

Where love comes alive™

SPOTLIGHT

"Delightful and delicious...Cindi Myers always satisfies!"

—*USA TODAY bestselling author Julie Ortolon*

National bestselling author

Cindi Myers

She's got more than it takes for
the six o'clock news...

Learning Curves

Tired of battling the image problems that her
size-twelve curves cause with her network news
job, Shelly Piper takes a position as co-anchor on
public television with Jack Halloran. But as they
work together on down-and-dirty hard-news
stories, all Shelly can think of is Jack!

Plus, exclusive bonus features inside!

On sale in October.

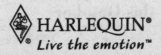

HARLEQUIN®
Live the emotion™